"Cole."

Ice filled Cole's chest. His lungs. His veins.

It would have frozen his heart if he'd had one—but the woman into whose enormous emerald eyes he was staring had stolen it from him long ago and ripped it to shreds.

"Tessa." Cole clenched his jaw and both fists. What kind of nightmare had he just stepped into?

"I—uh—" Tessa stammered, her wide-eyed, questioning gaze flashing from Cole to Alexis and then back to Cole again. "What are you doing here?"

That was exactly the question he wanted to ask her. But she'd asked him first. Her eyebrows rose as she waited for his answer.

"Workin'," he answered reluctantly, tapping his hat against his blue jeans.

"Here?" Her voice, which Cole remembered as soft and lilting, sounded scratchy and strained, much as he imagined his own voice did. "Alexis? Wh-what—"

"We've just hired Cole on as a wrangler now that he's moved back to town," Alexis explained, her tone overly bright. "Surprise!"

Deb Kastner is an award-winning author who lives and writes in beautiful Colorado. Since her daughters have grown into adulthood and her nest is almost empty, she is excited to be able to discover new adventures, challenges and blessings, the biggest of which are her sweet grandchildren. She enjoys reading, watching movies, listening to music, singing in the church choir, and attending concerts and musicals.

Books by Deb Kastner

Love Inspired

Cowboy Country

Yuletide Baby
The Cowboy's Forever Family
The Cowboy's Surprise Baby

Email Order Brides

Phoebe's Groom
The Doctor's Secret Son
The Nanny's Twin Blessings
Meeting Mr. Right

Serendipity Sweethearts

The Soldier's Sweetheart
Her Valentine Sheriff
Redeeming the Rancher

Visit the Author Profile page at Harlequin.com for more titles.

The Cowboy's Surprise Baby

Deb Kastner

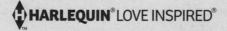

Recycling programs
for this product may
not exist in your area.

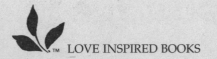 LOVE INSPIRED BOOKS

ISBN-13: 978-0-373-81852-5

The Cowboy's Surprise Baby

Copyright © 2015 by Debra Kastner

www.Harlequin.com

Printed in U.S.A.

And the King will answer and say to them,
"Assuredly, I say to you,
Inasmuch as you did it to one of the least of these
My brethren,
You did it to Me."
—*Matthew* 25:40

To my wonderful sister Amy for all her help in giving the horses in my book their unique names and personalities. Your animal sanctuary makes a real difference in the world!

Those interested in Amy's animal rescue program can find out more about Happy Haven Farm & Sanctuary on Facebook or at her website, happyhavenfarm.org.

Chapter One

Cole Bishop didn't know who'd originally coined the phrase "Home is where the heart is," but whoever it was, *she* should have been shot. Home was where the heart*break* was, and if it wasn't for the fact that his whole world was in an uproar, Cole would happily have never set foot in his hometown again for as long as he lived. Except maybe to visit his family, and there were ways to get around that obstacle.

Serendipity, Texas, was too small even to warrant a dot on the map, and its residents had minds like elephants and considered gossip a national pastime. He must be out of his mind for returning. His worst memories would be dredged up, and fast.

A man's got to do what he's got to do. For his son.

Truth was, he had nowhere else to go.

"Much obliged for the job." Cole nodded to Alexis Haddon of Redemption Ranch and curled the brim of his hat in his fist, tapping the dark brown Stetson against his thigh. He and Alexis had grown up together. When she'd heard he was back in town, she'd immediately contacted him to see if he wanted to work for her. And he was grateful. Now that he had a son, he needed steady employment more than ever, and wrangling sounded mighty good after years serving on an aircraft carrier in the navy. Less structure, more open space.

Alexis leaned her hip against the corner of her neatly organized desk and beamed at him with happy eyes and a white-toothed smile. Her husband, Griff, kicked back in the desk chair, lacing his fingers behind his head and admiring his wife.

"That's my Alexis. Always thinking of others."

Alexis laughed and waved him away. "Don't be silly." She turned her blue eyes on Cole and used the same hand to flick her long blond hair off her shoulders. "It's a privilege. As soon as I heard you were out of the navy and moving back to Serendipity, I knew

I had to snatch you up before some other ranch manager did."

It wasn't so much what Alexis had said, but something about the way she said it sent a ripple of forewarning down Cole's spine. He might have been imagining the feeling, except for the brief, surprised jerk of Griff's left eyebrow.

Cole swallowed hard. Something was brewing in Alexis's crafty female brain. He could see it in her eyes.

Whatever it was, Cole wanted nothing to do with it. His whole reason for accepting this position was to lose himself out on the range, where his biggest problems would be livestock and not people. With his background in naval intelligence, he was way overqualified for the job, but that was the whole point. He could be working for the CIA or FBI, but all he really wanted to do was spend time on the back of a horse. He had more than enough of a challenge learning to be a single father to Grayson without adding additional stress—or a job that would take him away from home or put him in danger.

He might not like it, but Serendipity was the right place to be, if for no other reason than that he had the support of his family here. And the community.

Alexis shot her husband a warning look before turning a warm smile on Cole. "As I was saying," she continued, sounding miffed, as if Griff had verbally interrupted her instead of merely questioning her with a look, "Griff and I both want to thank you for your military service and welcome you back home."

Cole gave an affirmative jerk of his chin. He never knew what to do or say when folks thanked him for his service to the country. He appreciated the sentiment, but it made him feel uncomfortable.

"I—er—" he stammered and then cleared his throat. He lifted his hat until it hovered over the general area of his heart in a gesture of respect. "Like I said before, I'm grateful for the position."

"And we're blessed to have you." Alexis glanced at her watch and then at the door as if she'd suddenly realized she had somewhere else to be.

Cole took that to mean they were finished. "I'll be off, then."

"Our first staff meeting of the month is tomorrow at 2:00 p.m. here at the house. It's casual—we meet around our dining room table. It'll be your first official shift."

"Glad to have this afternoon off. That'll give me a little bit of time to settle in at my dad's house." He nodded at Griff and Alexis. "He says he's happy to watch Grayson during the days for me, but it's a lot of change at once and a steep learning curve for all of us."

"The Lord will bless your sacrifice, Cole," Alexis said, patting his arm. "I can't imagine how difficult this must be for you, but I believe a baby is always a good and perfect gift from God."

Cole pressed his lips together and nodded. *Difficult* didn't even begin to describe his life since the moment he'd discovered he was going to be a father.

"Now, let me just run down your job description for you and we'll be all set," Alexis continued.

Cole exhaled as stress eased off his shoulders. He'd be wrangling. How hard could it be?

"Honey, don't you think we ought to mention—" Griff started to say, but he was interrupted by two sharp raps on the open office door.

Alexis's eyes widened to epic proportions,

and she caught her bottom lip in her teeth as if to stop herself from giggling. Griff's chair slammed upright.

A chill raced down Cole's spine and he turned on his heel.

"Alexis, I was looking over the background files for the incoming group of girls and it appears—" The auburn-haired woman's gaze rose from the pile of manila folders in her arms, and she gasped audibly.

"Cole." She frowned and raised the files in front of her like a shield.

Ice filled Cole's chest. His lungs. His veins.

It would have frozen his heart if he'd had one—but the woman into whose enormous emerald eyes he was staring had stolen it from him long ago and had ripped it into shreds. It remained beyond repair even all these years later.

"Tessa." Cole stiffened. He clenched his jaw and both fists.

He hadn't expected to find her in Serendipity, much less at Redemption Ranch. Tessa Applewhite worked *here*? After he'd just signed on to do the same?

What kind of nightmare had he just stepped into? He hadn't asked anyone about Tessa's whereabouts, of course, and he had good reason not to. Broaching the subject of Tessa with anyone in Serendipity would have dredged up memories he most definitely wanted to forget. Not to mention it would likely have set tongues wagging again, no matter who he asked.

"I—uh—" Tessa stammered, her wide-eyed, questioning gaze flashing from Cole to Alexis and then back to Cole again. "What are you doing here?"

That was exactly the question he wanted to ask her. What had happened to becoming a lawyer? He never imagined she'd return home. There wasn't much call for legal help in Serendipity, and the town's one lawyer more than covered it.

But she had asked him first. Her eyebrows rose as she waited for his answer.

"Workin'," he answered reluctantly, tapping his hat against his blue jeans.

"Here?" Her voice, which Cole remembered as soft and lilting, sounded scratchy and strained, much as he imagined his own voice did. "Alexis? W-what—"

"We've just hired Cole on as a wrangler now that he's moved back to town," Alexis explained, her tone overly bright. "Surprise!"

Cole cringed. *Surprise? Seriously?*

Is that what Alexis had been thinking when she'd offered him the job? That he and Tessa would be glad to see each other after all this time apart? That she'd be acting as some kind of matchmaker between the two of them?

That was the furthest thing from the truth, at least for Cole. And judging by the distress lining Tessa's features, he guessed she was feeling the same way.

No need to prolong the agony.

He planted his hat on his head and adjusted the brim, then tipped it to both of the women as his mama had taught him to do when he was a youngster. He'd always shown respect to the ladies, although at the moment he wasn't keen on being in the room with either one of them. "If you'll excuse me, I have things that need attending to."

Like his son. Even though every single part of being a new father, and a single dad at that, was excruciatingly difficult for Cole, it beat standing here eye to eye with the one woman in the world he least wanted to see right now.

Or ever.

He started toward the doorway, intending to slip past Tessa and be on his way, but when he started to go by her, her arm snaked out, her hand pressing against his chest.

"Cole, wait."

Even through the cotton of his T-shirt, her palm felt blistering hot, and he wanted to jerk away. It was only a final, slim shred of dignity and pride that held him back. Or at least that was what he kept telling himself. In truth, he wasn't certain he could have moved if he tried.

It should have been easy for him to keep walking. Tessa was a little wisp of a thing, and even had she given it her best shot, she could not have physically held him back. But when their gazes locked, no matter how loud his mind screamed for him to keep moving, his body refused to cooperate.

He couldn't catch a breath. His chest ached and his throat burned. His pulse roared and thundered in his ears.

From the corner of his eye, Cole saw Griff come out from behind the desk and take his wife's elbow. Clearly Alexis had schooled Griff on Cole and Tessa's rocky past. "Why don't we let these two have a moment alone together?"

It was more of a statement than a question, and although Alexis looked ready to argue, she wasn't allowed the opportunity to do so.

Griff herded her through the door, shooting an apologetic grin over his shoulder.

"Take as much time as you need." Griff closed the office door behind him.

Cole winced. He didn't need any time at all. Not one single second. He had nothing to say to Tessa. They might have had something to say to each other years ago, but now there was nothing.

Still, there was no sense standing in front of the closed door. He used his free hand to pry her palm from his chest, feeling as if it were glued there. He removed his hat and tossed it onto the desk, eyeing the chair Griff had vacated. At least that would put some distance between them—distance he desperately needed right now.

He'd thought all it would take to put Tessa behind him was time. Time and the distraction of serving on a United States Navy aircraft carrier.

But looking into her eyes, he might as well have been in high school all over again. His gut flipped and his head spun, just as they had when he'd been a foolish teenager who'd imagined himself in love.

What was *wrong* with him?

Tessa had caught him off guard, that's what it was. And then she'd gone and cornered him in this office. It was no wonder his thoughts were bouncing around like a loose racquetball in a closed court.

What did she expect him to say now that she had him penned in here?

Hey, how are you? What's been happening since we last saw each other?

He scoffed. He had nothing—*nothing*—to say to her.

He crossed his arms, rocked back on the heels of his boots and waited.

And waited.

Tessa looked equally uncomfortable, shifting her weight from foot to foot as her gaze darted everywhere except him. Tension mounted between them, the strain thick and palpable and tight as a wire.

He shook his head. She looked as if she didn't want to be here, and he most certainly did not. One of them was going to have to break the silence, and if she wasn't going to do it, then he would. Better to get this unexpected confrontation out of the way. He had much more important things to do than stand here waiting for her to collect her thoughts.

He narrowed his gaze, growling the question that was highest on his list.

"What do you want, Red?"

Tessa's heart skipped a beat and it was all she could do not to gape at him. She hadn't heard that nickname since the last time they'd been together. A lifetime had passed since then.

One look at Cole confirmed he felt the same. Gone was the smiling, blond young man whose luminescent blue eyes made her feel as if she was the most beautiful woman in the world and the only one for him.

In its place were hard angles, raw muscles, rough edges. He stood with his legs braced and his arms crossed over his massive chest in a universally defensive position. His gaze was cold and hard on hers, his scowl low and ominous. The tic in the corner of his jaw suggested he wasn't happy about waiting for her to answer his question.

Only she didn't *know* the answer. She'd been caught so completely off guard when her eyes had first met Cole's that every thought had flown from her head. He'd made no apology when he'd tried to excuse himself, clearly anxious to be rid of her. And for some reason she couldn't explain even to herself, she'd held him back.

What *did* she expect?

Nothing. Not from Cole Bishop.

Maybe it was the knee-jerk reaction of her more sensible, professional self, already trying to work out the sticky details of this new challenge. Better that than the sheer, foolish impulse on her part of wanting to be near him, if only for a few more seconds.

Nope. She'd go with the rational explanation.

As unfortunate as it might be, their lives had once more intersected. He was working at the ranch now, side by side with her. They'd be forced to interact with each other on an almost daily basis. She couldn't think of anything more potentially disastrous. With their history...

Sparks were bound to fly. And not the good kind, either.

"So you'll be wrangling here," she blurted out, a fact already confirmed by Alexis. But she had to start somewhere.

"Yep." His gaze narrowed even more.

Well, that was helpful. Tessa tried again.

"You've been discharged from the navy?"

He frowned and jammed his fists into the front pockets of his worn blue jeans. "Yep."

She was beyond frustrated at his cold reception, but she supposed she had it coming. She could hardly expect better when the last time they'd seen each other was—

Well, there was no use dwelling on the past. If Cole was going to work here with her, he would have to get over it.

So, for that matter, would she.

She'd always known there was the possibility Cole would return to Serendipity, but he'd made the navy his career, and she'd assumed that by the time they finally met again, they would both have moved on, would have had spouses and children. He must have returned to Serendipity a few times over the years to visit his family, but he'd obviously gone to great lengths to stay off her radar.

The fact that she hadn't been able to connect with any other man long-term was irrelevant—as was the way her heart had skidded the moment her eyes met Cole's.

"I was given to believe you were making a career out of the military," she said, alluding to the question she wanted to ask without really putting it out there.

"I was." His brow lowered. There was that

tic in his jaw again, the period at the end of his sentence. Clearly he didn't want to talk to her about himself or the navy, but the questions lingered in her mind.

Why hadn't he reenlisted at the end of this particular tour of duty? Why had he left the service before he had enough years to draw a pension? What had changed?

She had no right to ask.

But this standoff, or whatever it was, just wasn't going to work for them. Even if they walked away today without resolving anything, there would be tomorrow—and the next day, and the day after that. Did he not realize they would be interacting with each other on a frequent basis during each of the Mission Months?

"You do know we have to work together?" She couldn't help it if her question sounded acerbic.

He shrugged. "I don't see why. You're not a wrangler."

It wasn't a question, exactly, but at least he was talking, so she decided to answer, anyway. "No. No, I'm not. I'm a counselor, actually."

"A what?"

"Redemption Ranch isn't exactly a cattle

operation. Well, there is plenty of stock to care for, as I'm sure you've seen, but there's much more going on around here than that. Alexis brings in youth who've gotten into minor trouble with the law. Instead of community service cleaning trash off the highways, they come here to learn honest work and real love."

Those words sounded wonderful and positive in theory. If only they worked out so well in practice—but they didn't. Not always. She would have liked to think she made a difference in the girls' lives, but sometimes everything she gave just wasn't enough.

"Juvenile delinquents?"

Tessa chuckled. "That's one way of putting it."

"I don't get it." He shoved his fingers through his thick blond hair and shook his head. "I thought you wanted to be a lawyer."

"Daddy wanted me to be a lawyer." That was a topic for a different discussion, and she wasn't going to get into that with him now. "When I went to college, I discovered my real interest lay in psychology. I received my master's degree and then returned to Serendipity to work here at Redemption Ranch."

"Why?"

"Why did I choose psychology?"

"Why did you come back to Serendipity?"

"I never intended to leave Serendipity in the first place. I thought you knew that."

His eyes clouded with confusion but quickly froze to an ice blue.

"You were the one who wanted to leave," she pointed out. She hadn't realized that at the time, when they were dating as teenagers. She should have seen the signs, but didn't, hadn't heard what he was trying to tell her. Cole had thought the navy would be a way of escaping what, to a restless teenage boy, must have seemed like a dull and dreary existence. The polar opposite of what her heart ached for. As an army brat who'd never known a sense of community before she and her father had landed in Serendipity, Tessa had been, and still was, on the totally opposite end of *that* spectrum. She loved what Serendipity offered.

Just as she hadn't realized the depth of his desire to leave, Cole hadn't recognized her need for stability in her life—something the military couldn't offer. He'd wanted to take her with him on his worldwide adventure. *Planned* to take her with him, in fact. As his wife.

Wow, had they ever gotten their wires crossed. Talk about a serious lack of communication.

But back then, they'd both been immature teenagers with their heads in the clouds, floating along on the wings of love. Now their feet were on solid, unforgiving ground, anchored there by the weight of reality.

"Still seems to me it won't be hard to avoid each other," he said, his voice gravelly.

Especially if we're trying.

It was what he'd left unspoken that stung her emotions like the crack of a whip. Well, he didn't need to get so personal. And he was still laboring under a mistaken impression about how often they would have to be in each other's company.

"I take it Alexis hasn't run down your job description with you yet. She hasn't shared the particulars of what the wranglers are expected to do here?"

He scoffed. "We were interrupted before we could finish our conversation," he reminded her with a bite to his tone. "Anyway, what's to know? I've been riding and roping since before I could walk. Not like I need on-the-job training or anything."

"Yes, but—" She started to tell him that the wrangling he'd be doing at Redemption

Ranch had much more to do with the teenagers than it did with the cattle, but it wasn't really her place to inform him of his official job description.

Who knew? Maybe Alexis had something different in mind for Cole—something that wouldn't require them to suffer through the perpetual awkwardness Tessa knew would remain between them.

"Well, I won't keep you," she said, reaching back to open the office door. "I just wanted to make sure we had an understanding about how our professional relationship here at the ranch was going to go."

He scowled at the word *relationship* and slammed his dark brown Stetson on his head.

"Just came as a surprise, is all," he muttered.

"I'll say," Tessa agreed.

"Didn't expect to be back in Serendipity for a few years yet. Maybe ever."

He sounded so bitter that Tessa cringed. What had happened to the boy she'd once known? Who or what had darkened the sunshine that had once shone so brilliantly in his eyes?

"Cole? Why did you come back now?" She knew she was taking a mighty big risk asking such a personal question, but it seemed to her that he'd been the one to open the door to the subject. She held her breath and waited for an answer.

He tipped his hat and started to walk past her without speaking, and Tessa thought she'd pushed him too far. Whatever his issues were, they were his business, and clearly she was the last person on earth he'd talk to about them even if he was inclined to share.

He was almost out the door when he suddenly swiveled around to face her.

"Grayson." His gaze narrowed on her as if weighing the effect of his words on her.

She scrambled to put his answer in some kind of context but came up with nothing.

"Who—"

He cut off her question and ground out the rest of his answer.

"My son."

Chapter Two

Yesterday at the Haddons' office, after throwing the curveball that emotionally knocked Tessa right off the mound, Cole had walked away without another word.

She walked down the row of pinewood beds within the girls' dorm, absently making small corrections to the square corners of the sheets as she went. The room was silent and empty now, but tomorrow morning it would be filled with the chitter-chattering of adolescent females, none of them happy about being pawned off into Tessa's care. At least, at first they wouldn't be. Tessa's experience was that the young ladies under her supervision eventually adapted, and she liked to think they left Redemption Ranch better people than when they first arrived.

Now that it was morning, she was bone-weary from lack of sleep and from fighting all the emotions stirred up by Cole's unexpected pronouncement.

Cole had a son?

Probably a wife as well, although he hadn't mentioned her.

He had a *family.*

She let the thought sink in, rest for a moment deep in her chest until her breath evened out.

Why had his news taken her so very much by surprise? It shouldn't have, and she was a little ashamed by her lack of forethought and her response. Just because *she* was single and unattached didn't mean Cole wouldn't have found someone to settle down and share his life with. That the thought hadn't even occurred to her at the time explained why she'd been shaken up.

She needed to get her head together. Her newest young charges were arriving for their Mission Month tomorrow, and she had to make sure everything was ready for them. A stab of pain and regret sliced through her gut. She prayed every day that she'd make a real difference in the teenage girls' lives, but no matter how hard she tried, no matter what she did, it wasn't always enough. Her mind strayed for a brief moment to Savannah, a girl who'd visited the ranch last summer. Savannah had shown a great deal of promise during her stay. Her attitude, once bitter and angry, melted under Tessa's tender love and direction. By the time Savannah left, Tessa was certain she was destined for a better future.

She'd been wrong. Shortly after leaving Redemption Ranch, Savannah had become pregnant, and her parents had thrown her out on the street. Tessa had lost track of her then. She didn't know what had happened to Savannah or her precious baby.

Being the female counselor at the ranch, Tessa was responsible for her teenage girls nearly twenty-four-seven during what the Haddons termed their Mission Months. Ten months a year with little breathing space between groups of kids. It was a hard position to be in and a heavy load to carry, yet Tessa's heart was completely in her work. She softly whispered another prayer for the six young ladies who'd soon be arriving, asking that this time she'd reach them all.

She groaned and pushed her hair off her forehead with the palm of her hand. If only it were so easy to push the melancholy thoughts from her mind.

Focus.

The humidity was even higher than usual today, and her long, thick locks were unwieldy on the best of days. As a youngster she'd been teased about her frizzy red mop, and she'd always been self-conscious about her hair— until a blue-eyed boy with a smile that could melt glaciers came into her life and made her feel like the most beautiful woman in the world, both inside and out.

When Cole had first coined the nickname *Red*, he had made it sound like the best kind of compliment, his own special name for her, said with the utmost affection. She hadn't dreamed such love existed—at least not for her. Even as a boy, Cole had changed everything for her.

But yesterday when she'd wandered into the Haddons' office with her mind on the incoming teenagers, she'd discovered that boy had become a man.

And *Red*?

Uttered from his frowning lips and tight jaw, the word no longer sounded like a compliment.

Cole was hardly recognizable from the youth

he'd once been. He'd sprung up several more inches in height. His shoulders had broadened and his voice had deepened. His skin was weathered. He was clearly a man who spent his time outdoors.

But it wasn't so much the physical changes that had shocked her most. It was his attitude, his bitterness, the ice in his gaze. While it felt as if his emotions were gathered in his eyes and flung right at her, she knew he couldn't possibly still be carrying *that* big a grudge against her. Yes, she'd hurt him. She would be the first to admit that. But too many years had passed since then. She couldn't put her finger on it, but there was…something else. What had happened to him that had put such a big chip on his shoulder?

Whatever it was, it wasn't any of her business. He had a family now.

She refused to acknowledge any hurt that went along with that news. Why should it bother her? Her feelings for Cole had long since been carefully packaged away, deep in the recesses of her heart. She rarely even revisited them anymore. Mostly. Except for those rare instances when loneliness overtook her and the dark of night stretched before her.

She snorted and rolled her eyes at her own foolishness. When had she become so melodramatic?

"Are you okay?" The smooth tenor voice of her friend Marcus Ender, the male counselor at the ranch, came from behind her.

Tessa hadn't heard him come in, and she jumped in surprise.

"Don't do that to me, you jerk," she admonished him good-naturedly, laying a hand over her hammering heart. "And to answer your question, yes, I'm fine."

She attempted to paste a smile on her face, but Marcus tilted his head and cocked one dark blond eyebrow.

"Now, why don't I believe that? Come on, Tessa. I've known you too long for you to try to pull one over on me. You look like you've seen a ghost."

She swallowed air and nearly choked on it. "To be entirely truthful with you, I kind of have."

Marcus's other brow darted up to join the first.

"Cole Bishop is in town."

Tessa and Marcus had known each other since their undergraduate years, when they were both pursuing psychology degrees, and had been good friends ever since. He knew the whole sad story about what had happened between her and Cole and the way things had been left when they parted.

"Oh, wow," Marcus replied with a low whistle. "Do you know how long he's staying? Is he here on leave to visit his family?"

Her throat hitched. "No. He's back for good. He's got a son—a family. And the worst of it is that Alexis hired him to work at the ranch."

"Seriously? Why would she do that? Doesn't she know the history between you and Cole?"

"That's the odd thing. Alexis knows exactly what happened between us. She was there when it all played out."

Along with every other resident of Serendipity.

He shook his head. "I can't imagine what she was thinkin'. Then again, I've never been very good at interpreting the female mind." He crossed his eyes and flashed a goofy grin.

Despite everything weighing her down, Tessa laughed. Marcus always knew how to make her feel better.

"Speaking of female minds, why don't we try to get you out of yours for a while? I'm running into town to get a few things from

Emerson's Hardware before we have the staff meeting this afternoon. You want to come along?"

She hesitated, pursing her lips. "I don't know. I won't be very good company."

"What if I bribed you with one of Phoebe Hawkins's red velvet cupcakes from Cup O' Jo's? Smothered in chocolate frosting?"

"A cupcake? And my favorite? You're not playing fair."

"When have I ever?" he tossed back with a wink.

Tessa knew he was right. She tended to overanalyze every situation, and this one was a humdinger. There were things a woman could change and things she couldn't, and there was no sense worrying about what was out of her control. At the end of the day, the good Lord had the final say. That's what she often told the girls she was counseling, and yet now she was struggling to take her own advice.

Emerson's Hardware, only a few minutes from Redemption Ranch, was located on Main Street, right next door to Cup O' Jo's Café. All of Main Street looked like something out of an old Western movie, with colorful clapboard siding and old-fashioned signs dangling in front of the stores.

While Marcus dawdled in the hardware section, Tessa wandered over to gardening to see what was new. Living in the girls' bunkhouse as she did, she had neither the place nor the time for a garden, but she imagined that someday, when she had a home of her own, she'd enjoy planting vegetables and spending quiet time landscaping with flowers around the place.

When she had a home of her own.

Realistically, was that ever going to happen?

What a difference a day made, if that day meant Cole Bishop had walked back into her life. Even the thought of having a family now tore at her heart. What was once a pleasant, if distant, dream of the future had suddenly become a nightmare. She hadn't realized until she'd seen him again that he'd still been part of her vision. His face had never been replaced by another.

Shaking her head to dislodge her sadness, she found Marcus at the register, where he was wrapping up his purchase.

Edward Emerson, an older man dressed in the same bib overalls as the two men slouched in the wooden rocking chairs just outside the door, smiled at her as she approached.

"Hey, Tessa. Good to see you. Can you do me a favor and tell Cole the feed he ordered is loaded in his truck and ready to go whenever he is?"

"I... I don't—" she stammered, but Edward went on as if she hadn't spoken.

"If I'm not mistaken, he's at Cup O' Jo's showing off that new baby of his. Cute little tyke. Bald as a cue ball." Edward chuckled.

Tessa inhaled sharply. Cole's son was an infant. Her stomach churned like a combine at hearing the news, creating a whole new set of aches. Her thoughts flew together like a tornado picking up everything in its path. Thoughts that didn't belong together but still tore through her. Her failure with Savannah was too recent, and Savannah's baby was never far from her mind. She'd once thought she'd be the one bearing Cole's children. But now Cole had a son of his own, and his and Tessa's lives were completely separated.

She had to pull herself together, and fast. Cole had just become a father, and he'd come back to settle down. It made perfect sense. He had moved on, and so had she. And yet she had no desire to find Cole right now, not when it meant she was going to have to meet his family. She was *so* not prepared for that moment. Not right now.

Not ever.

"We'd be glad to," Marcus answered for her, giving her a friendly nudge with his shoulder.

"I'm not ready," she whispered hoarsely as they exited the store. "Did you hear that? Cole's son is a baby. I can't— It's not—"

Marcus knew about Savannah, understood about Cole, and she could tell from his gaze that he knew where all her thoughts were flying. He reached for her elbow and pulled her to a stop on the clapboard sidewalk.

"Better now than later, Tessa," he insisted. "It's not gonna get any easier for you if you wait on this thing. I know you. You'll noodle it over and over again until you've built it into a giant issue. In a situation like this, the best thing you can do is face your fear and rip it off like a bandage. It'll hurt less in the long run."

She made a face at him. "When did you become so smart?"

He laughed. "I'm an expert, remember? I have the degree hangin' on my wall to prove it."

She sighed. She hated to admit it, but Marcus was probably right. Might as well get it over with now. She couldn't avoid Cole and his family forever.

Even so, she hesitated a beat at the entrance to the café.

"Bandage," Marcus reminded her, using his palm to press her forward from the small of her back.

The inside of Cup O' Jo's was a stark contrast to the outside. Filled with the delicious scents of home-style cooking and fresh pastries, the whole place had the look and feel of a modern coffee shop. There were even computers lining the back wall so folks could access the internet.

It was immediately obvious where Cole and his family were located. Practically everyone in the café hovered around one of the middle tables, their exclamations ranging from "Ooh" and "Aww" to "What a little cutie-pie" and "Sweet darlin'."

Jo Spencer, the owner of the café, looked up and waved Tessa and Marcus over. Her red curls bobbed as she placed a hand over her heart and bounced on her toes.

"Cole's back in town," she said, her voice rising with excitement. "And my stars. Have you seen Baby Grayson?"

Tessa nodded to acknowledge the fact that

she knew Cole was back in town and then shook her head. "I haven't met Grayson yet."

"Come, come," Jo insisted, dragging Tessa by the hand. Tessa shot a flustered glance over her shoulder, but Marcus just shrugged and grinned, mouthing the word *bandage.*

Insensitive jerk. He was going to be no help at all.

Now that she was under Jo's guidance, Tessa knew she had no hope whatsoever of backing out of the situation. There was no arguing with the woman once the vivacious old lady got something into her head.

Besides, what would Tessa say? That she didn't want to see the baby?

How would that sound? Everyone loved babies.

She did, too, of course. It was this particular baby at this exact time she was struggling with. Her emotions were screaming for her to flee. She didn't think her heart could stand glimpsing the infant who was bound to carry at least some of Cole's strong features. And was the child's mother present? That would cause Tessa even more heartache.

Marcus was wrong. She *wasn't* ready yet, and getting caught in a situation where she might break down emotionally wasn't ripping off the bandage. It was creating a whole new wound.

Panic welled in her chest, and her pulse pounded in her temple.

Not yet. Not yet. Not yet, it echoed.

The crowd parted like the Red Sea in front of Moses as she approached, probably half out of deference to Jo and half due to the distinct possibility of drama between Cole and Tessa. Serendipity townsfolk liked nothing quite so much as a scene that might as well have been taken right out of a soap opera.

She took a deep breath and plunged forward. If they were waiting for drama, they were going to have to wait a good long time.

She got her first look at Cole, who held his loosely swaddled son in the crook of one arm. The baby's tiny fist was wrapped around one of Cole's thumbs. He looked to be only a few weeks old, incredibly small against Cole's large chest and muscular biceps, and yet the big man was holding the baby with such infinite tenderness, it brought a hitch to Tessa's throat. Cole was beaming with pride as he showed off his boy. He was meant to be a father.

Tessa gasped for air and coached herself to breathe normally. If she hyperventilated and passed out, that would really be a show for the neighbors. She plastered her best smile on her face and stepped into the center of the circle. It seemed as if her whole relationship with Cole had been in the public eye, from their quite literally dramatic start on the theatrical stage in high school to the dreadful finish on yet another stage, when she'd painfully but unavoidably ruined any future between them. She would not and could not break down now, not with so many of her neighbors and friends looking on.

Cole's eyes widened when he saw her. His brow lowered and the smile dropped from his lips—until the infant moved in his arms. The stiffness to Cole's shoulders remained, but when his gaze dropped back to his son, there was only love and awe in his expression.

Cole was a daddy. A proud papa to his little bundle of joy. How right he looked filling that role.

He cleared his throat, his jaw tightening with strain once again. He appeared to be considering his thoughts, weighing his options. After a long pause, he spoke softly so as not to disturb the baby. Tessa was keenly aware that his voice lost its angry edge in deference to the child.

"Everyone else here has already had a turn. You want to hold him?"

She sat down in the nearest chair and swallowed her shock as Cole held his son out to her, gently settling the infant in her arms, his fingers brushing hers as he rearranged her hand to cradle the child better.

Grayson had been noisily sucking on his two middle fingers, but when he looked up at Tessa, he popped his fingers out of his mouth and smiled and cooed at her. As Edward had said, the baby didn't have a lick of hair, but his eyes were the exact color of Cole's, and he had his nose and the twin crescents of dimples in his cheeks.

Tessa's heart welled until she thought it might burst. It was the worst and most awful concoction of pleasure and pain she'd ever experienced. Why was Cole doing this, letting her hold his precious baby?

Because others were watching? Did he really have no idea how badly this would hurt her, this stark, physical reminder of what might have been if she hadn't rejected his marriage proposal? Or was that exactly what he was trying to do?

She searched his gaze but found nothing to condemn him, and the upward curve of his lips suggested little other than the satisfaction he'd found in becoming a dad. But his voice was low and gravelly when he finally spoke, the only indication his emotions were stronger than he was feigning.

"Tessa, I'd like you to meet my son, Grayson."

It just figured that Tessa would show up at Cup O' Jo's right as Cole was out giving the community their first glimpse of Grayson. He'd gone out with his son this morning before the staff meeting on purpose, believing Tessa would be otherwise engaged, back at the ranch getting ready for her teenagers to arrive.

As if that in itself wasn't complicated enough, old friends and neighbors crowded around him, taking up his breathing space and giving rise to all kinds of questions and speculations. Like what had happened to Grayson's mother, and how was he coping with being a single dad.

That was enough stress. More than enough. The last thing he needed was for Tessa to walk in the door with some strange cowboy Cole didn't recognize. Serendipity had remained remarkably unchanged throughout the years he'd been gone, but it had definitely changed some.

Even so, he was confident he could rely on the community. They would have a keen interest in the details, but they also had open hearts with which to embrace him and his son. It wasn't surprising that everyone would want to know the story of how he'd happened back into town with a baby in tow and no wife to speak of. Most, like Jo, wouldn't allow him to skim through an explanation. He'd rather not delve back into his shameful past.

He was a single father. He'd stepped up, and that was all that really mattered. End of story.

After that first burst of surprise and panic when Tessa walked in the door, his mind had fled him completely. He hadn't been thinking—which was the only possible explanation for why he'd passed Grayson into Tessa's arms. Moving back to Serendipity, he had no intention for Tessa to interact with his son, but his pride and ego had flared up at the sight of her, and the offer had come barreling out of his mouth without his say-so.

His emotions, slow to catch up, had exploded in his chest, razor-sharp shards puncturing his heart and lungs. Tessa smiled as she gazed down at the infant. Her cheeks blushed a sweet peach, and joy radiated from her expression. Her rich alto softened into a melodious Texan lilt as she spoke a series of adorable nonsense words to Grayson.

Grayson had been a regular fussbudget earlier when Cole had allowed each of his neighbors the opportunity to hold the baby. He'd howled and wailed and protested with his little fists until he was once again in the comfort and security of his daddy's arms.

But with Tessa, Grayson was an entirely different child. Cole's throat tightened until he couldn't catch a breath as his son babbled happily at Tessa, perfectly at ease in her arms. When Tessa smiled at Grayson, the baby beamed back at her, and the ache in Cole's chest deepened. Grayson had *smiled* for Tessa with no more than her little bit of coaxing. Cole wished it was easier to get that kind of response from his son. He felt as if he had to work for every little thing, and it all seemed to come so easy for Tessa. A natural mother if there ever was one.

Jealousy snapped and burned in Cole's gut. That smile was supposed to be for *him*. Whether or not she'd meant to, she'd stolen something from him, and he could barely withhold his frustration.

"Well, would you look at that," Jo said, leaning over Tessa's shoulder so she could get a better look at Grayson. "The little fellow has really taken to you, Tessa. You were born to be a mother, my dear. You'll make a great one someday."

So she wasn't yet a mother? Until this moment, he'd been so caught up in his own problems that it hadn't even occurred to him other things might have changed during his time away from Serendipity. He surreptitiously glanced at Tessa's left hand.

No ring.

Not that it mattered if she was married or not. The point was that she hadn't wanted to be married to *him*.

Cole didn't miss the cringe that rippled across Tessa's shoulders at Jo's words, or the frown that pursed her full lips as her panicked gaze flashed from Cole to the fellow she'd come in with. Her expression lasted only for a split second, and she recovered nicely with a smile that probably fooled nearly everyone in the room. It didn't work on Cole, though.

Her guy friend seemed to think a grin and a wink would solve her problems.

Cole knew better.

Even after all these years, he could read Tessa like a book. Every happy smile, heart-rending frown, radiant beam of joy and scowl of frustration. And while Cole knew she was genuinely enjoying her interactions with Grayson, the rest of it was all an act. She didn't want to be here any more than he wanted her to be.

They were at the mother of all standoffs, unable to back down even if they wanted to. Living in the same small town. Working at the same ranch. The never-ending possibility of being thrown together at social events.

Would it ever get any easier for him to be around her? Would he ever not *hurt* when he looked at her?

The plethora of emotions he was experiencing today, battling through him with a vengeance, were just as mercilessly and excruciatingly painful as they had been when he'd first seen Tessa in the Haddons' office. It was all he could do to stay put and keep his game face on. Pretty much every nerve in his body was screaming to snatch Grayson up and head for the hills as fast as his legs would carry him.

That ought to set tongues to wagging.

Tessa had broken his heart so completely that he had burned through the stages of grief not once, but every single year since that day. For years, the first Saturday of June had tortured him with memories—only now it was far worse than just a recollection.

Tessa was sitting there alive and in person, right in line with his gaze, rocking his baby, looking exactly the way he'd always pictured she would when they started a family together.

Jo was right. Tessa was a natural mama if there ever was one—but then, Cole had always known she would be.

Only Grayson wasn't her baby.

And Cole couldn't stand one more second of this torture. He had to get out now, before his emotions got the better of him. Because the only thing worse than what he was feeling right now would be for Tessa—not to mention the whole community gathered around him—to see just how far he had fallen.

"Time to give my little cowboy a diaper change," he muttered. Anything to get the baby out of Tessa's arms. He reached for Grayson, intending to make a quick exit, but Jo was too fast for him.

"Now wait just one moment, dear. I'm ashamed to say we don't yet have a portable changing table in the men's restroom. Never even gave it a second thought until now. I promise y'all that particular item has just been bumped to the top of my to-do list."

"Oh. I—uh—" After seven weeks he would have thought he could work out simple issues like this, but he kept stumbling upon new ones. Where did a single man change a baby's diaper in a small-town café?

During the first few weeks, when he'd been settling the legal paperwork between him and the baby's mother, he'd lodged with a navy buddy, Emilio Gonzalez, and his wife, Ella. He'd appreciated spending time with Ella, who was an experienced mother of six and a wonderful, patient teacher. Having a woman's touch around was invaluable, in more ways than he cared to count. Truthfully, he'd let poor Ella do much of the work. He realized in hindsight that he should have been throwing himself into learning the ropes as he had in the navy. Watching and doing were hardly the same thing.

Cole sighed inwardly. Grayson would be better off if he had a woman's influence in his life, and Cole silently acknowledged that he needed the help. But that was not reality for him and Grayson, and it might not ever be. He was on his own, and he'd never felt as powerless as he did in that moment, with everyone's eyes on him.

A little help here, Lord, he prayed silently.

"You don't have to leave on account of Gray's diaper," Jo assured him. "The ladies' room is fully equipped. Tessa, would you do the honors? Where's your diaper bag, son?" She directed her first question to Tessa and her second to Cole. Her eyes were sparkling with mischief and Cole cringed. Good ol' Jo, ever the matchmaker.

He pointed to the giraffe-print bag on a nearby table. Jo dug through the bag for a diaper and wipes while Cole shifted his gaze to Tessa. She looked like a cornered wild animal, her eyes darting around the room as if looking for a quick way to escape.

In any other situation, he might have found the whole thing amusing, but there was not one single thing funny about having to share breathing space with Tessa, much less having her commandeer his baby, even if it was only for a diaper change.

"You've never changed a baby before?" he guessed, his lips quirking. Even on her worst day, she couldn't be half as inept as he'd been his first few go-rounds, but he would shoot himself before he ever admitted that aloud.

Her auburn eyebrows hit her hairline. "It… it's not that. I don't mind changing Grayson for you. I've had my fair share of experience handling babies now and again. I was just wondering—that is—is your wife around? I don't think we've met."

Of course. Tessa didn't know he wasn't married. He'd hoped that particular tidbit would make its way around town and he'd never have to encounter that question. It was just like Tessa to have avoided the gossip. He wondered what people were saying, exactly. Folks were going to make all the wrong assumptions unless he set them straight. In a down-home, conservative little Texas town like Serendipity, things were done right and in the proper order.

First comes love, then comes marriage, and *then* comes the baby in the baby carriage.

Only that's not how it had been for Cole. To his everlasting shame, Grayson wasn't the product of love *or* marriage. That didn't mean Cole didn't love his son with all his heart. Grayson was far and away the biggest blessing God had ever given him. He had such awe and wonder about this new little human being. The curve of Grayson's ears, his fingers and toes, the way the baby already responded to Cole's voice in the dead of night when it was just the two of them awake and rocking to a lullaby.

It might not have happened the way he

would have planned, but it had happened, and being a father to Grayson was Cole's new mission, more important than anything he'd done in the navy. More important than anything he'd ever done in his *life*.

He was not proud of how he'd gotten to this point, but he was proud of being here, of being Grayson's father. As for his son's mother...

"I'm not married," he admitted softly, sliding his chair closer to hers so they wouldn't be overheard.

Tessa's brow rose again, and Cole frowned. She didn't have to gape. This didn't bode well for how the rest of the town was going to take the news.

"I see," she murmured.

No, she didn't. She hadn't a clue about the man he'd become. He wasn't the bright-eyed kid who'd dated her all through high school. Not even close.

"I don't want to talk about it," he said.

"I'm sorry." Her tone was punctuated with bitterness. "I had no right to ask."

She was taking it personally. This wasn't personal. It had nothing to do with her at all. "You couldn't have known."

"I'll just— Let me go take care of his diaper

real fast for you, and then you can have the baby back," she stammered.

He watched her make a quick exit into the ladies' room, the sweet, fruity scent of her perfume lingering behind her. He blew out a frustrated breath and threaded his fingers through his hair.

He was quick to acknowledge his own part in his disaster of a life, but he had faith that the Lord would use it for good, even if he didn't have any idea how that might work out for him, or for Grayson. He could only put himself and his baby in God's capable hands.

He didn't know why the Lord had set him on this path, but he imagined he must be even more hardheaded than he'd realized. Most horses could be broken with a whisper. It appeared he needed the sharp jerk of a bit to get him moving in the right direction.

When Tessa returned with his still-happy infant, she immediately deposited Grayson into Cole's arms. He adjusted his son to his shoulder and gently patted his back.

"After I saw Grayson was with you, I completely spaced on the reason I came to Cup O' Jo's in the first place," she admitted with a forced chuckle.

"A cupcake?" Tessa's friend stepped into

Cole's line of vision and dropped into the conversation as if he belonged there. "Here's temptation for you." He waved the chocolate-iced cupcake under Tessa's nose.

Red velvet.

Even though Cole couldn't see what the chocolate icing was hiding, he was absolutely certain of it. Tessa had always been partial to red velvet with chocolate frosting. He personally thought it was an odd combination—a whipped white cream cheese frosting suited him fine—but he'd always humored her.

She made a face at the man. "You get a pass for abandoning me back there, but only because of the cupcake."

Tessa's friend turned a winsome smile on Cole that seemed a little over the top, given the circumstances. He ought to save his charm for the ladies. But when he extended his hand, Cole had no choice but to respond.

"I'm Marcus Ender, by the way. Boys' counselor at Redemption Ranch."

Cole shifted Grayson so he could meet the man's hand with his own. He might have been guilty of adding a little extra pressure to his grip, but a handshake told a lot about a man. Surprise flashed in Marcus's gaze at the strength of Cole's grip, but he didn't break the contact until Cole did.

A challenge? Marcus's gaze said it all. He was looking out for his friend, and Cole had better not hurt her. Cole tempered his naturally aggressive response. He couldn't fault Tessa's friend's overprotective instincts, he supposed. Marcus didn't have any way of knowing Cole would never hurt Tessa. Not intentionally, anyway.

"I'm Cole—"

"Bishop," Marcus finished for him. "Yeah. I know."

And he didn't sound too thrilled about it, either.

Cole's hackles rose, and the hair on his neck stood on end. What exactly had Tessa told Marcus about him?

It couldn't be good. He was probably better off not knowing. But it rankled him nevertheless.

Grayson whimpered in protest as Cole's arm tightened.

"Sorry, little man," he murmured in the baby's ear.

"Red? You were saying?" he reminded Tessa. "Why you came over to Cup O' Jo's in the first place?"

"Red?" Marcus snorted and burst into laughter, but it instantly died when he was simultaneously punctured by both Cole's and Tessa's glares. He held up his hands in a sign of surrender.

"I was over at Emerson's before I came here," Tessa explained. "Edward asked me to give you a message."

Cole relaxed his stance, rocking back on the heels of his boots. He hadn't realized how tense he'd been since Tessa had walked into the café, and all this time it had been about a feed order.

If his day could get messed up this quickly just by the sight and scent of Tessa, he didn't have a prayer of ever truly settling down and making a life here.

"The feed's ready?" he offered, hoping to stay within comfortable bounds of conversation.

"All loaded up in your pickup and ready to go."

He pressed a breath from his lungs. "Thanks for the heads-up. I think poor Grayson here has had about as much doting and loving from the community as he can handle for one day."

Grayson? Forget the baby. *Cole's* head was whirling.

His gaze met Tessa's, and he could see she was thinking the same thing.

First time out of the chute. No score.

Cole cleared his throat. "Best be getting home. It's about Gray's nap time."

"Right, okay," Tessa agreed with a smile that didn't reach her eyes. "I guess Marcus and I will see you later, at the meeting."

Tessa blended into the crowd, and Cole reached for the handle of the giraffe diaper bag, slipping it onto his shoulder. Even after all these weeks, it still felt odd to him to tote around a bag that was similar to a woman's purse. Chalk that one up to necessity—diapers, wipes, bottles, pacifiers, toys. He tried to ignore the way the bag tromped all over his masculinity.

"Are you leaving?" Jo bustled up to Cole and reached for his bicep. "Can you wait just one more moment, dear?"

Cole nodded, but he tensed when Jo made a beeline toward Tessa, who was speaking to Dr. Delia and her husband, Zach. Jo linked elbows with Tessa and drew her back in Cole's direction.

"If I could have a quick word with the two of you?"

What now?

Tension rippled across Cole's shoulders and down his spine. Jo Spencer was the nicest woman a man could know, but she was also a little bit scheming when it came to matchmaking. She had a bird's-eye view from her spot behind the counter of Cup O' Jo's, and she tended to see what was what—or who should be with whom—far before the rest of Serendipity caught on.

Well, as long as it wasn't matchmaking, Cole would be all right with whatever Jo had in mind.

"Alexis and I were talkin' about the upcoming summer barbecue."

Electricity bolted through him at Jo's words. His gaze locked with Tessa's. She looked every bit as shocked as he felt.

Not the June BBQ. Anything but that.

"She was telling me she'd like to see the teens get involved this year. We usually relegate them to set up and clean up, and I suggested that they might want to do something different this year—entertainment. The band we contracted with backed out on us. Slade and Samantha have pulled together some musicians for dancing, but Alexis really wanted the kids to do something special for the townsfolk, give them a little show. Do you think you two could get together and work something up for us? A scene from a musical, perhaps? The planning committee would sure appreciate your efforts, my dears."

Was she kidding? A scene from a musical? No *way* was that going to happen. Cole and Tessa had first met—first *kissed*—performing a scene from a musical. And they had broken up at the June BBQ. The beginning and the end of their relationship.

Cole had no intention of helping those kids do anything, musical or otherwise. Working with delinquent teenagers wasn't even in his skill set. Besides, he wasn't going to the barbecue, much less participating in it.

"Why don't you ask Marcus?" he suggested through gritted teeth. "He's the boys' counselor, after all. He ought to be the one leading this thing, don't you think?"

Jo barked out a laugh. Even Tessa chuckled.

"Honey, that man cannot carry a tune for a second, much less an entire musical number. He's as tone-deaf as a rock. As I recall, you have a beautiful baritone voice. Surely you'll step up and share your talent for the good of the community—and the teenagers."

Jo was goading him—and she was good at it. He remembered all the many times growing up when she'd set him on the right path. Part of him instinctively reacted as if he were still a child, but he was a grown man now, and he had no intention of being pushed into a situation that would be nothing but trouble for him, and for Tessa, too.

Why wasn't *she* speaking up?

"We'll see what we can do," Tessa said.

What?

"Great! Can't wait to see what you two come up with." Jo scuttled away before he gave his own answer—which would have been a *no*. He didn't even have the opportunity to raise another objection, not that Jo would have listened to it.

Cole leaned into Tessa's personal space, meeting her emerald-eyed gaze square on. "What are you thinking?" he demanded. "You know as well as I do that we can't *do* this."

"I admit it's not ideal."

"Not *ideal*? It's plain crazy."

Tessa sighed. "We would have given in eventually. You know Jo. I just saved us having to scrap with her."

He hated that Tessa was right. Jo would have won in the end, stubborn woman that she was. But how could they get over… *everything*…to work together in such a capacity? At the moment he couldn't even go there in his mind.

"I can't see how this is going to work," he muttered crossly.

"That makes two of us. But it has to happen, Cole. We have to put our differences aside for the sake of the teenagers. They deserve the chance to do something good and to experience the community's positive response to their actions."

Honestly, his mind wasn't on the teenagers. It was on himself and his own discomfort. Was this the Lord's design to give him the opportunity to step out in faith—and completely out of his comfort zone? If it was, it was way, *way* out.

Right out of the frying pan and straight into the fire.

Chapter Three

Tessa straightened her color-coordinated file folders, one for each of the incoming teenagers, and laid them atop a lavender-colored three-ring binder, in which she kept all her additional notes. At the moment, she was the only one sitting at the Haddons' dining room table.

Early as usual.

She usually took the extra time before the meeting to pray for the incoming teenagers and quiet her heart so she would be open to whatever new challenges lay ahead, but after what had happened earlier in the day at Cup O' Jo's, she couldn't get her mind or her emotions to stop buzzing around like a hive of angry wasps. Unlike bees, which stung once and died, wasps had the capacity to sting over and over again.

Cole was a single father.

While that explained a lot, it still filled her with confusion. No wonder he'd returned to Serendipity. He was bound to need the help of his family and friends to raise Grayson. She imagined it was hard to go it alone. He was blessed to have his brother Eli and sister Vee and their spouses living close by. Plenty of aunts and uncles to spoil little Grayson.

She couldn't help but wonder how the whole *single dad* part of it had come to be. That wasn't the sort of information a man shared with an ex-girlfriend, especially one with whom he'd had such a conspicuous breakup.

Single mothers, as heartbreaking as they were, were a dime a dozen given the current society. One mistake and they were the ones left holding the baby, the ones whose whole lives were forever changed in an instant. The men—they could walk away. It might be wrong, but that's how it was. They could choose whether or not to be responsible for their child.

Cole, apparently, had made that noble decision.

Her first instinct would be to think he was a widower, but that wasn't what he'd said. He'd said he wasn't married. Not that he had been married, or that he was divorced. He *wasn't* married.

Which meant what?

She didn't know, and really, she shouldn't want to know. She needed to keep her attention where it belonged—on her career and her incoming charges—and mind her own business where Cole was concerned. She wasn't even *close* to being ready to work with Cole on the musical number with the teenagers, so she pressed that problem as far back in her mind as she could force it.

She scoffed and flipped open the hot-pink folder on the top of the pile, then glanced down and read the name on the file. Kaylie Johnson. Fifteen. Had been picked up for underage drinking and arguing with a police officer. Obstructing justice. Not a smart move, but a fairly typical case. Most of the teenagers came to the ranch with a chip on their shoulders. It was her job to provide the tough love that usually turned the kids around—a combination of counseling and good, hard physical labor. Redemption Ranch was the perfect place to keep teenage hands and minds busy.

And if God was gracious, Tessa hoped her own mind would be likewise occupied. She longed to be too tired to think, to drop into bed at night without any dreams. Busy enough for the ever-present thoughts of a blue-eyed cowboy to be overshadowed.

Unfortunately, she couldn't get away from him in her thoughts or in person, because Cole arrived a moment later, hat in hand, his thick blond hair windswept and messy. She was a little surprised to see him arrive early to the meeting. She remembered him as being chronically late to class and church when they were in high school.

Their eyes met, and Tessa noticed something she'd overlooked when she'd seen him at Cup O' Jo's. The pitiable man had dark circles under his eyes and a rough-lined, haggard expression that suggested he hadn't been getting enough sleep. Had he been keeping late nights with the baby?

"Does Grayson have his days and nights mixed up?" she asked, gesturing to the chair opposite her. Any discomfort that she might feel being alone with him was offset by how thoroughly exhausted he looked. The kind thing for her to do would be to hold off on the snark she usually used in defensive mode. She really did feel sorry for him—a little. Besides, Marcus and the Haddons couldn't be far behind. A glance at her watch told her there were only five minutes to spare.

Cole groaned as he slid into his chair. "We had Grayson pretty well set on a schedule in California, but the move messed him up again, poor little guy."

Tessa's breath caught. "We?"

"The folks I stayed with while I worked out the legal issues with Grayson. They were such a blessing."

She wanted to ask him about the legal issues he'd been facing. Instead, she said, "That was very kind of them."

"I'll say. I had a lot to learn about baby care."

"I can only imagine." Truthfully, Tessa didn't really know. She'd been around her friends' babies on occasion, but taking care of an infant twenty-four-seven, and as a single parent at that—well, that was a horse of a different color. No wonder Cole's skin looked a little pasty.

Tessa rolled her eyes at the sound of clamoring and clunking coming from the front room. She didn't have to turn around to know it was Marcus—the man was built like a giant and moved with all the grace of a bull in a china shop, no matter where he was.

"Oh, good. I'm not late, then," Marcus said, dropping into the chair next to Tessa and slinging an arm along the back of her chair.

Marcus grinned at Cole, who narrowed his gaze on the spot where Marcus's shoulder touched Tessa's. Part of her wanted to correct the mistaken impression Cole might be getting, but then again, why should she bother? It wasn't like it mattered.

"That's got to be some kind of record for you, Marcus," she quipped back. She was joking, but not entirely inaccurately. Marcus did tend to show up late to the staff meetings. He had his own sense of timing—casual, cool, no worries. Chill. His kind of attitude drove on-time and organized Tessa nuts.

"So what have you got there, *Red*?" Marcus asked, grinning and emphasizing the last word. He gestured toward her pile of file folders and then slapped his own onto the table, all a generic manila.

Red.

The name made Tessa's stomach churn, as if she'd eaten something that disagreed with her. Cole's pet name for her didn't belong in this conversation, most especially on Marcus's lips. It was sure to get Cole's goat. They all had to find a way to work together. Didn't Marcus have a brain in that head of his?

Probably not. Marcus was the kind of man who used his looks and charm to get his way and thought everything in life was easy if it was faced with a smile.

But he'd crossed a line here, right into Cole's territory. She scowled at Marcus in an unspoken warning. Goading Cole was not a good idea. Ever. He would most certainly lose that battle.

Don't do it.

Then her gaze flashed to Cole, half feeling she owed him an explanation or apology for Marcus's airheaded slip of the tongue, but Cole's gaze was on Marcus's and the meaning in his expression was clear.

Leave it be. Cole frowned and looked as if he wanted to say something. Tessa looked back at Marcus, feeling panicked.

Fortunately, Tessa was saved from having to ply the men physically off each other by the appearance of Alexis and Griff. Griff seemed to be unaware of the overabundance of testosterone crackling through the room, but Alexis raised an eyebrow as she surveyed the men glaring at each other across the table.

One corner of Alexis's mouth turned up,

and she tilted her head at Tessa, asking for an explanation without speaking a word, her eyes sparkling with mischief.

Tessa shrugged. How was she supposed to know why the two men were apparently at odds with each other? If she could read the male mind, maybe she could have staved off a few of her past mistakes. Maybe she and Cole—

Alexis looked from Marcus to Cole and then back to Tessa, chuckling and winking. Tessa didn't even want to know what kind of conclusions Alexis had just made and she failed to see how the situation was humorous.

It was wrong.

Just *wrong*—on so many levels.

"Where are the rest of the wranglers?" Cole asked, shattering the tension with his deep voice. Apparently he'd chosen to be the better man and back down, although the aggression in his eyes hadn't lightened.

Everyone's gaze snapped to him.

He cleared his throat. "I'm kinda feeling like the odd man out here. Did I misunderstand my directions?"

Alexis slid into the chair at the head of the table, and Griff seated himself at the foot. Alexis leaned her elbows against the polished oak, steepling her fingers under her chin. "No, you're supposed to be here today. No confusion. But in answer to your question, you're it, Cole, where the wranglers are concerned. Today, anyway. We sometimes meet with the whole wrangling crew, but most often our monthly Mission meetings are just Griff and me and the counselors. Oh—and occasionally the board of directors and any townsfolk who want to get involved. We've got some interesting programs developing here."

"Okay," he said, drawing out the word. His gaze clouded with confusion and he ran a hand across the stubble on his jaw.

"We've got only a few men working the ranch aspect of the ministry. The other guys have been wrangling for us for a while now, so they know what's expected of them," Griff explained. "We've asked you to join us today because—" he paused and shot a meaningful look at Tessa "—we were interrupted the other day before we could get to the heart of what we do here. And we thought you might like to have a glimpse of what happens behind the scenes here at the ranch. I have a lot of faith in you, Cole, and I'd like you to take a more active role in this ministry."

Cole's eyes widened to epic proportions. It

was all Tessa could do not to chuckle. Not *at* him—despite everything that had passed between them, she couldn't help but respect everything the man was trying to do to juggle his responsibilities as a father.

"I'm not sure what you mean. You've clearly got the wrong fellow. I'm not a *ministry* kind of guy," he said, kicking up one side of his lips into the magnetic half smile that used to send a kaleidoscope of butterflies swirling through Tessa's stomach. Now it was all she could do to swallow the tender outpouring of emotions that whirled through her.

"I'm familiar with all aspects of ranching and don't mind hard work," he continued. "You can put me wherever you need me, and I'll come through for you. Just point me in the right direction." It was what he didn't say that hung in the air.

Tessa held her breath. Her heart swelled at the strength of purpose in Cole's voice. His intensity and honor were part of what had so attracted her to him in the first place, even back when they'd been nothing more than a couple of immature high school students.

Now Cole wore his strength and potency like a cloak around him, his posture straight and his shoulders squared. Teenagers could use strong leadership in their lives. Cole would be good for this ministry. He just didn't know it yet.

"Of course, you'll be assisting the other wranglers with the daily chores around the ranch and taking care of the stock," Alexis agreed. "That part of your job description will be right in your comfort zone. I'm sure you've noticed we have a variety of animals here at the ranch."

Cole nodded briskly, but his expression remained guarded. Everyone in the room could hear the *but* that was about to follow, and Cole was no exception. Tessa watched a wave of tension roll over his shoulders and a scowl briefly line his face before he schooled it.

Alexis either didn't notice the tautness in the air or had decided to slice through it with her words. "*But* though caring for the animals is one of the conditions of the job for the wranglers around here, Redemption Ranch isn't exactly a working ranch, not in the typical sense of the word. The stock we keep here at the ranch is mostly for the teenagers to learn from and interact with."

"Tessa told me a little bit about that." The corner of his jaw ticked with strain. Tessa suspected he could guess what was coming next. He'd already been railroaded into working with her and the teenagers for the barbecue. Now he was about to find out he had even more responsibilities where the kids were concerned.

"I would have hit that subject in more detail the other day, except—" The end of Alexis's sentence dropped into an uneasy silence.

The tension in the air was palpable as everyone waited for Alexis to finish her thought.

"There are—um—trail rides." Alexis's voice had risen sharply and came out as a bit of a squeak, and no wonder.

Cole was a true cowboy, and trail rides were…not so much. There was absolutely no comparison, a grown man tending to what he would consider a bunch of squawking adolescents, most of whom knew zero about horses and frankly had a negative mindset about life in general and horsemanship in particular. The city kids didn't know anything about horses and really didn't want to know, and it would be Cole's assignment to ignore their attitudes and walk them around at a sluggish plod, their horses head to tail with the next.

Tessa couldn't see how that would work out well for anybody. Cole was a man who craved excitement. He'd bucked bareback through high school rodeo and seen the world on board a naval cruiser. Even when he'd taken an afternoon job wrangling cattle in his youth, he'd had more than his fair share of moments when he would get to ride like the wind. The slow pace of trail rides would be like a death sentence to the active cowboy, and as for working with the teenagers, Tessa couldn't imagine that to be high on his bucket list.

It was as if Alexis was trying to sandwich the unfamiliar and no doubt unwanted duty between those with which Cole was comfortable. Not that he'd be *comfortable* interacting with the teenagers in any regard, but she suspected teaching ranch life and how to care for the animals would be superior to leading trail rides, at least in Cole's mind.

"We need you to ride along with us to make sure all the kids are following their safety rules."

It took Cole a moment to respond. "Like a dude ranch, you mean?"

Tessa wasn't overly surprised that he didn't sound too enthused about the prospect.

"You want me to load the kids up on horses, lead them out on the trail and show them some of the property. Make them feel like real cowboys." He shrugged. "All right. I guess I can do that," he said with a conceding wave of his arm.

"Well…" Griff hedged.

Cole arched his left eyebrow. "There's more?"

"Yeah, there's more. We don't run Redemption Ranch exactly like a dude ranch," Griff said. "We're hoping you'll take up *all* the challenges inherent in your position. You'll be interacting with the teenagers on trail rides—" He paused and cleared his throat. "And then some. Our hope is that you'll find both challenge and pleasure showing the youth what ranch life is all about, helping them connect with God and the country."

Cole's gaze widened noticeably, but Griff continued, either unaware of the shift of tension in the room or choosing to ignore Cole's obvious discomfort.

"We're putting you in charge of overseeing their ranch discovery outings. You'll be responsible for leading them in their interactions with the animals, teaching them the care and feeding of the stock, how to tack up a horse and other aspects of country living. It's an interesting position that I think you'll enjoy once you get used to the idea. I can guarantee it will be the most rewarding work you've ever done."

Cole shook his head. Tessa couldn't imagine how he felt right now. He was no doubt still overwhelmed in his new role as a single father, and now Alexis and Griff were throwing delinquent teenagers at him.

"Think of it as an art," Alexis encouraged him. "Very few of these kids have been within arm's length of a horse. You'll be starting from scratch and can make true horsemen and women out of them."

Cole's brow furrowed, and he shoved his fingers through his hair, rubbing at the knots at the back of his skull. Tessa linked her fingers in her lap, trying not to remember the times she'd rubbed the knots from his neck when he was facing a tough test or a new challenge. He'd always been muscular, but years in the navy had defined the muscles in his shoulders and arms. Just for a moment, before reality reclaimed her, she ached to ease his tension, even after all these years and all that had transpired between them. She shook her head, nipping her misplaced wistfulness in the bud.

"You'll be a wonderful mentor," Alexis assured him. "You have so much to give. The kids will be blessed, and I believe you will be, as well. That's why I was so quick to snap you up once I knew you were coming home."

Cole's neck turned red, then his chin, his cheeks, his forehead, until there wasn't an inch on his face that wasn't flushed. "I think you've got this all wrong. I'm a simple cowboy, not a teacher. Yes, I joined the navy, but those skills don't transfer to this kind of situation. And I didn't even go to college. I couldn't teach a fly, much less a teenager."

Everyone around the table laughed—except for Tessa and Cole.

"Maybe not," Marcus said, which earned him a glare. Marcus just brushed it off. "But it sounds to me like you've got some skills. You're going to be a music teacher to these kids, right?"

Tessa cringed. No matter what her personal differences were with Cole, she didn't think it was fair for everyone to be sharing a laugh at his expense. Clearly the man was ruffled, and why wouldn't he be? He'd been expecting the somewhat reserved and quiet life of a wrangler out on the open Texas plains, probably a welcome change from his navy days. Instead, he was getting herded into what must seem like babysitting a group of juvenile delinquents—which wasn't all that far from the truth. The one thing she *could* guarantee was that it would be anything but calm and peaceful.

It was her fault he was only learning this now and not when he'd first accepted the job. She'd interrupted him that day and thrown everyone's world off-kilter.

Without thinking, she reached across the table and laid her hand on Cole's forearm. It was as muscular and strong as she remembered it. Even more so. "I know it might sound overwhelming to you right now, but trust me on this—working with young people and knowing you're making a difference in their lives—well, there's no better feeling in the world. You're going to be a real *mentor* to these kids, Cole. Think of all the teenagers you'll be able to help by sharing your skills and expertise with them."

Cole shook his head, and she knew from the way the muscles in his forearm tensed that he was on the brink of bowing out entirely. Jobs were scarce in Serendipity, but she was certain he'd be hired on somewhere, either wrangling or else using whatever skills he'd learned in his years as a sailor—and he wouldn't have to deal with a bunch of juvenile delinquents.

Teenagers weren't everyone's cup of tea. And he did have a lot on his plate as it was.

She knew without a doubt there would be something for him. He'd been born and raised in Serendipity. The townsfolk wouldn't turn their backs on one of their own, especially not one with a baby to love and care for.

"I know it sounds like a bit much," Alexis added, "and I apologize that I've had to drop it on you so suddenly, but I want you to know I sincerely believe in the reason I've asked you to work here and specifically in this capacity. I don't ask lightly. I've prayed about it, and I truly feel you're the right man for the job."

His gaze widened, but instead of looking at Alexis, his eyes landed on Tessa. She couldn't help but think that the next words out of his mouth were going to be about her—or at least because of her.

"Yeah—no. I'm sorry, but I don't think so."

And she was right.

A *mentor*?

Alexis thought he could be a mentor? To a bunch of impressionable teenagers? How blind was she? Not to mention everyone else sitting at the table with him. They were all acting as if he was something special, as if he could add to the team in some positive way.

What were they seeing that he wasn't? Because when he looked in the mirror, all he saw was a rough-edged cowboy-slash-sailor who'd made more mistakes in his life than he could count—*major* mistakes. Errors that would affect some people's lives—like Grayson's—forever. Cole didn't want a teenager looking at *his* life as an example of how to live. He wasn't someone *any* parent would want around their children.

Anyway, wasn't that what the counselors were for?

Despite the fact that his heart had never healed toward her, he knew Tessa to be the kind of woman a teenager would be smart to emulate. He'd fallen in love with her for a reason. She was as intelligent as she was beautiful, and she had a kind and compassionate spirit that benefited everyone she came into contact with.

Well, everyone except for him. But that was between the two of them. It didn't have a thing to do with the work—the ministry—she was a part of now.

As for Marcus Ender, Cole didn't trust the man as far as he could throw him, but again, that was for personal reasons. For all he knew, the same traits that made his hair prickle were the same ones that made Marcus a great counselor.

Whatever. The only thing Cole knew for sure was that *he* wasn't anything close to mentor material. It was bad enough that he'd been strong-armed to help prepare the kids for some kind of musical number for a barbecue he didn't even want to attend. But this was too much.

"Hey, look," he said, holding his hand out palm up and offering an apologetic shrug, "I appreciate what y'all are trying to do here for me. I do. But me and kids? We don't mix all that well. I've had zero experience with teenagers. And to be perfectly honest with you, I've already got my hands full with Grayson."

"That's true," Alexis admitted. "There's a learning curve when it comes to teenagers, but no more so than with babies. And it appears to me you are adjusting quite nicely with your son. I have high hopes for you here."

Griff barked out a laugh. "My wife is making it sound like you can kill two birds with one stone. Take what you learn with the baby and apply it to the teenagers."

"And who's to say you can't?" Alexis jabbed back in a teasing tone of voice.

"Not helping," Tessa mumbled, pressing her free palm to her forehead.

The movement caught Cole's attention, and it was only then that he realized her other hand still rested on his arm. He snatched his forearm away from her touch as if she'd bitten it and clenched his fists in his lap.

His dander rose at her comment. Tessa hadn't spoken loudly enough for anyone except him to hear, but what she'd said still cut to the core of his ego. Maybe internally he acknowledged that his learning curve on babies was tighter than a hairpin turn on a mountain road, but Tessa didn't have to agree with him. If his success rate with Grayson was anything to go by, he'd never be able to figure out how to help a teenager, and it sounded as if they expected him to be very involved in the process.

Mentor.

That was a big word.

"We'll start you off easy," Alexis assured him. "The teens arrive tomorrow, and then we've got a trail ride scheduled for the morning after. Nothing fancy. You can take the time between now and then to familiarize yourself with the land and pick a route you'd like to take. Or ask any of the other wranglers, and they can suggest something for you."

Cole nodded and cleared his throat, feeling as if he should be rejecting this agreement but finding himself completely without words. It didn't matter what he said, anyway. He wasn't going to be able to walk away now. Not and keep his dignity.

"There are twelve kids in this lot, nine of whom have indicated they have never ridden a horse before, so you'll want to keep that in mind when you're selecting their mounts. You'll need to get acquainted with our stable full of horses. Most of our stock are so gentle a toddler could ride them—or in this case, a city kid who has never seen a real live horse before, which, trust me, is close to the same thing."

"Sometimes worse," Marcus joked.

Cole ignored Marcus and his attempt to be witty. His gaze widened on Alexis as she pelted directions at him. How was he going to remember all this?

As if she could read his mind—or maybe his expression—Tessa tore a few pages of yellow paper from her legal pad and handed them to him, then clicked a blue pen open and tossed it his direction.

Thankfully his reflexes worked faster than his brain, and he caught the pen with no problem. That was all he needed, to have the thing bounce off the table so he'd have to crawl around on the floor to get it. It was bad enough that Marcus had his eye on him, but the one who really mattered was Tessa.

He'd thought he'd reached the very dregs of personal humiliation with Tessa many years ago, before he'd left for the navy, but now that he was back in town and in front of her again, he had to wonder. Would the awkwardness between them dim with time? Was she even feeling the tension and chemistry inherent between them, or was it all in his imagination?

Probably. He scoffed at himself.

Pulling his mind back to the task at hand, he scribbled a few notes about what Alexis had said. At least she'd paused so he could catch up.

"We own twenty horses in addition to those owned by the wranglers and counselors. You're welcome to board your own horse here, as well. I know it's going to take some time for you to get to know the idiosyncrasies of each of the mounts, but I have every confidence that you'll be able to match up the right horses with the right teenagers."

"It's as much about the attitudes of the youths as it is their riding abilities or the temperament of a particular horse," Tessa explained.

Cole remembered once being responsible for choosing Tessa a mount from Serendipity's public stable, the very first time she'd ever ridden a horse in her life. He'd been the one to teach her, and they'd spent many hours together exploring the countryside. She'd apparently continued riding after he left, if she was now in possession of her own horse.

His chest tightened. A lot of time had passed since their dating days. He experienced the odd sensation of a gap, the lost time, opening like a large black cavern before him.

So much in Serendipity had stayed the same, and yet so much had changed.

Tessa had changed.

"I know horses," he admitted. "But how am I supposed to know what the kids are going to be like, much less what kind of ride to give them?"

Tessa and Marcus burst out laughing simultaneously.

"Trust me," said Marcus with the annoying

grin of his that Cole wanted to wipe off his face, "you'll know."

"They tend to wear their emotions on their sleeves," Tessa explained. "Five minutes in their presence and you'll know exactly which horse goes with which teenager."

Great.

He had his doubts that the boys would even try to be straight with him, especially given that they were all delinquents. They'd try to pull a fast one on him, and he suspected their attitudes might make teaching them to ride more complicated than it needed to be.

Then there were the girls, whom he could easily imagine overloaded with emotions. He wasn't so old and removed from civilian life that he didn't remember what happened when a bunch of teenage girls got together. Bubbly young ladies and skittish horses really did not mix. The very thought made him shiver. He was the last person in the world who wanted to deal with the racket created by a bunch of young women, with or without adding horses to the equation.

He groaned inwardly as his dream of losing himself on the peace and quiet of the range floated right out the window. Instead, he was supposed to be a *mentor*. Alexis and Griff clearly thought it was possible, but he still had his doubts.

"What about my hours?" he asked, tapping his pen against the table just to have something to do with his hands.

"We know you have a sweet little baby to go home to," Alexis said. "You'll have office hours, so to speak, and your weekends will be free to spend with Grayson. We'll have some of the other wranglers cover those shifts for you."

"I appreciate the consideration, but you really don't have to do that," Cole said. "Grayson is in good hands. I don't mind evening and weekend work when it's called for. I want to carry my weight around here."

"And you will. We all understand that your baby comes first," Alexis insisted. "It's no bother."

"That's the way we want it to be," Tessa agreed, compassion softening her voice. "The way it should be for a single parent. At the very least."

Cole swallowed hard.

"Be sure to let your father know he can contact you at any time, for any reason. On your cell phone, or he can reach us at the office, either way. It doesn't have to be an emergency."

"Your father?" Tessa echoed, arching her auburn brows.

"Dad is taking care of Grayson while I work."

"I was wondering who would—" She stammered to a halt. "I mean, that's incredibly generous of him."

"You've got that right. I wanted to hire a nanny, but Gramps, as he calls himself, wouldn't hear of anything else. He's over the moon to have a grandson and says he wants to spend every second with him."

Tessa chuckled, but her expression was a little sad. Cole's father had always treated her like a daughter, at least until their bad breakup. He'd never asked his dad about it, but he suspected she and Pop weren't on speaking terms now. Not after she'd publically humiliated Cole and left his heart in shreds.

Tessa shook her head and appeared to recover. Cole refused to acknowledge the warmth in his chest that accompanied the reappearance of her smile.

"So you really think I can do this?" he asked, directing his question to no one in particular. "This mentoring thing?"

"It's mostly a matter of practice," Tessa

assured him. "You'll be surprised how fast you pick up the nuances of teen-speak."

"Yeah, but y'all have a degree. I'm just a wrangler."

"A degree is neither here nor there," Griff said. "And besides, you're way more than just a wrangler, Cole. You're a sailor, too. I'm guessing you learned a great deal in the navy. College isn't the only way to learn about life. You've overcome obstacles in your past."

Yeah. By running away.

Cole quickly shifted his gaze away from Tessa lest she read on his face what he was thinking. The biggest obstacle of his life was sitting right across the table from him, and he couldn't say with any certainty that he'd *overcome* anything.

He focused on Griff. "Yes, sir, but nothing that's going to help me in this situation. The navy didn't give me a clue on how to wrangle a herd of rambunctious kids." He tried to make it sound like a joke, even if it wasn't.

"We'll ease you into it," Alexis promised, although from the smug look on Marcus's face and the distressed expression on Tessa's, he wasn't sure he believed Alexis's words. "Let's just start with the trail ride and see how you do. We're not leaving you on your own, you know. We'll all be along for the ride, so to speak."

Griff chuckled. "Literally speaking, she means."

Be that as it may, part of him wanted to get up right now and walk out of the room, even if that meant being without a job. The whole situation was *way* out of his comfort zone. But at one time in his life he'd chosen to run away to escape his problems, and he'd promised himself he would never do so again. He would face this challenge and conquer it.

Besides, this wasn't just about him. He had a son to provide for now. Griff and Alexis were offering him the flexibility of hours he needed in order to care for Grayson.

"Guess I'm up for a little adventure," he said reluctantly, punctuating his sentence with a nod. He swallowed around the apprehension clogging his throat. "Trail rides and teenagers."

And working with *Tessa*—which he knew would be the biggest challenge of them all.

Chapter Four

Tessa walked her palomino quarter horse gelding out of the barn and into the corral and haphazardly slung the lead around the split-rail fence. It was more habit than anything else. It wasn't necessary for her to tether Little Bit. Her horse had a remarkably easy and gentle spirit, and Tessa knew he could be depended on to stand steady while she tightened the cinch and swung into the saddle.

If only her emotions would behave as her horse did—stable and reliable instead of flitting off in every which direction.

If only Cole hadn't come back to town.

She'd purchased Little Bit as a gift to herself after she'd been at Redemption Ranch for a year. *To me, from me, because I love me,* she used to joke to Marcus. She adored riding and often chose to spend time in the saddle on her rare evenings off. It was one of her favorite perks of country living.

Back when she'd first arrived in Serendipity, she'd been an introverted army brat who'd never been within touching distance of a horse. Learning to ride had been a dream of hers, and Cole had made that dream come true. He'd become her whole world as he gave up his afternoons to teach her everything she now knew about horsemanship. She'd instantly taken to the majestic animals under Cole's gentle guidance, and to this day she remembered the smile on his face when he complimented her on how quickly she'd picked up the skills. As with everything else he'd done for her and with her, he'd treated her with tenderness, love and respect.

She sighed softly as memories overtook her. She and Cole had spent many happy hours in the saddle exploring the Texas plains. Racing across the grassy fields, enjoying the fresh air and the colorful wildflowers. Laughing with wholehearted abandon. Eagerly speaking of their combined hopes and dreams of what was to come, of spending their lives together. She'd been so certain their love would endure forever. Was it that long ago she'd imagined her future with Cole shining as brightly as the sun?

Though Cole had been her first serious boyfriend, she'd been thoroughly convinced he was her one and only true love. In her innocence of the way the world really worked, it had been incredibly simple back then for her to picture their lives forever entwined. Engagement. Marriage. A family. Gray hair. Growing old together, linked hand in hand until death did them part. Cliché, maybe, but her heart's desire nonetheless. Or at least it had been.

Then in one single moment, her once shiny world had turned as dark as a thunderstorm. And the truth was, she'd never quite gotten past the clouds. She didn't believe in fairy tales anymore. Her heart burned in an agonizing heat as those memories washed over her, and with them, the realization that the young man Cole once was no longer existed.

At least she'd finally been able to fulfill one heartfelt dream in her life—having a horse of her own. Before she'd permanently returned to Serendipity and gotten the job at Redemption Ranch, she'd put her love of horses aside to focus on her studies. Owning a horse wouldn't have been practical even if she'd had the time to ride, which she hadn't. Even when she'd returned home to Serendipity after college, her heart had tangled with the mixed memories of Cole and horses, the shades of white and black that swirled together whenever she thought of either one. It had taken her some time to get over those emotional imprints.

But when the Haddons had generously offered their stable and pastures to her as part of her employment package, how could she resist? She supposed it was God's perfect timing. Though the melancholy never quite went away, trail rides with Little Bit had become something to which she always looked forward.

Except today.

She usually tacked up in the stable, but today she'd taken Little Bit into the corral simply because she couldn't bear to be in the same room as Cole—even if the room in question was a barn, and even if he was busy saddling a dozen horses for the teenagers to use during the trail ride.

Echoing from inside the barn, she could hear Alexis lecturing the kids on trail ride etiquette, giving Tessa a moment to touch base with God before mounting up. As she usually did before any of the teens' activities, she offered up a prayer for the kids, but this time she asked for extra grace for herself, too. She had a feeling this wouldn't be a normal day for her in any regard—not with Cole along. It was going to be all she could do to tamp down the memories she knew would rise to the surface the moment she saw Cole on the back of a horse again. She was already struggling enough as it was.

In general, trail rides weren't especially noteworthy events, despite the protests that were even now forthcoming from some of the mouthier teens. At the beginning of their tenure, the teens seemed to think every event was worth a good grumble or two. At first it had concerned her, but now she'd experienced enough Mission Months to know that their complaints, loud as they were, were mostly guff and hot air. The boys, especially, liked to strut their stuff and act like tough guys, covering their vulnerabilities with a ramped-up bad-boy facade—and showing off for the young ladies.

Trail rides were an important part of the kids' rehabilitation. As a rule, the youth of both sexes were fascinated by the horses, whether they immediately cared to admit it or not. In Tessa's experience, she'd often found that the best kind of therapy for some of the teenagers was working with and caring for the equines assigned to them. Giving them the opportunity to nurture their horses not only gave them a sense of responsibility they often lacked in their daily lives at home but also afforded them the delight of discovery when their horses responded in turn. As Tessa well knew from her own encounters the bond between a horse and a human was both powerful and enchanting.

Tessa ran a hand down Little Bit's muzzle and breathed in the tangy blend of horse, hay and saddle leather that settled her heart in a way few other scents did.

"I think I may be in need of a little bit of therapy myself," she said aloud and then laughed at her own unwitting joke. "Pun not intended."

Little Bit snorted and threw his head as if he was nodding.

"I know, right? I'm absolutely hopeless."

"I could have told you that," said Marcus, leading his mount next to hers and flipping the stirrup out of the way in order to tighten the cinch on his mount. "I'm sure Little Bit agrees with me. Sissy, too. Right, girl?"

he asked, running his hand across the bay mare's flank.

"Shut up, you." She rolled her eyes. "Only you would name your horse Nemesis and then go and call her Sissy."

Marcus made a face at her, and she chuckled in response.

At least Cole hadn't been the one to discover her talking out loud to her horse. That would have been...worse than being caught by Marcus. Mortifying, actually. She could only imagine what Cole would think if he'd heard her admit to needing therapy, even if it was only in jest, and only to an animal who couldn't share the information. The last thing she wanted to do was give him an indication that his return to Serendipity affected her in *any* way.

Nothing like chasing trouble.

She mounted Little Bit and walked him around in a tight circle as she waited for the teenagers to make their way into the corral. The first ride always took the most preparation as the kids learned the basics of tacking up and mounting up. On their first day at the ranch, they'd been exposed to the *back end* responsibilities of caring for their assigned mounts—mucking stalls was always the first job Alexis assigned to the teenagers. The point was to get them acclimated to country life, she said, to shock their systems so they'd be ready to learn.

Equine boot camp, so to speak. And quite effective.

Tessa nudged Little Bit out of the way as Alexis led the first of the twelve teens out of the barn. A dark-haired young man named Caleb was clearly trying to look as if he rode horses every day. It was just as obvious to anyone in the know that he'd never been on a horse in his life. He clutched the saddle horn with white-knuckled hands as if it were a lifeline, and he was swaying loosely from side to side even though his mount was barely at a walk. His feet flopped all over the place despite being in the stirrups. An accidental trot and the kid would go flying.

Tessa reined Little Bit into position to keep Caleb's mount in place until the others were ready. She quietly gave him a few hints to stabilize his weight in the saddle. As Alexis returned to the barn, Cole led the next teenager out, Kaylie, a spindly, pretty little blonde dressed in jeggings and a blouse two sizes too big for her. The young lady probably swam in a size one.

Tessa shook her head. She couldn't believe how reed-thin teenage girls kept themselves these days. A stout burst of wind would blow Kaylie away. And by the end of the trail ride, she would regret wearing jeggings instead of good, solid denim. Tessa made a mental note to add that to her pretrail ride instructions for future groups. Designer jeans were bad enough, but jeggings? Spandex and saddle leather wouldn't mix for long, and Kaylie was bound to find herself saddle sore by the end of the ride, poor girl.

Marcus left Sissy tethered to the fence and helped Cole and Alexis lead the rest of the teens and their horses out one by one and line them up in a row. After a few minutes, all of the horses were out in the corral, the lead ropes were secured onto the saddles and the adults had mounted.

Tessa did everything she could to keep from looking at Cole. She gave various teenagers tips on technique. She counted backward from one hundred. But despite her best efforts, she found her gaze drifting his way. Her breath caught at the picture he made on the back of his horse. He still rode the same Appaloosa gelding he'd had in high school—Spot Check, nicknamed Checkers. She'd always admired how he looked in the saddle—like a cowboy out of an old Western. The way he rode was simply magnificent, man and horse moving as one unit. Back when they'd been dating, she'd never tired of watching him gallop across golden prairie grass.

Cole chose that moment to look in her direction, and their gazes locked. Her heart clenched in her throat, and for a few seconds it was as if the break between them had never happened. Everything else seemed to fade away. Only the two of them were here now, just as it had been back then.

Connected. Happy. Fulfilled.

"Listen up," Alexis called, gathering the teenagers' attention and whipping into Tessa's consciousness, causing her to jerk inadvertently on Little Bit's reins and send him into a half rear. Cole's blue eyes narrowed on her and then shifted away. She felt the loss intensely and only with effort turned her mind to gaining control over her horse and focusing on what Alexis was saying to the kids.

"I expect you to remember everything we've been over this morning. You'll be riding single file. No doubling up. Nose to tail, but be sure to leave room between your horse and the one in front of you. I don't care how capable you think you are as a rider—no funny stuff. No goofing around in the saddle. No wandering off the trail. Anyone who doesn't follow the rules gets KP duty for a week. You'll be responsible for the worst chores I can throw at you."

As Alexis continued her speech, Tessa walked Little Bit around the corral, checking to make sure each rider appeared securely balanced in the saddle and whispering suggestions and encouragement to the teenagers whenever she saw errors in form.

"I'll be leading this little expedition today," Alexis continued. "As we're exiting the corral, Marcus will direct you. Don't move until he tells you to, and pay special attention until we're all out on the trail. Cole and Tessa will be bringing up the rear and watching to make sure you're all safe and following the rules."

Cole frowned, clearly not any more enthused by Alexis's directions than Tessa was. Her stomach churned.

What was this about? There was more going on here than was immediately evident. Alexis wasn't making any sense patterning them this way. They'd never before used two adults following up at the back of the long parade of horses. In any other ride, she or Cole would be joining Marcus riding up and down the line.

It would make more *sense* to keep Cole and Tessa as far away from each other as possible. Like on different planets, perhaps.

Why was Alexis making things complicated? Surely she had to know how awkward they would feel.

Or maybe that was the whole point—intentionally pushing them together so they would be forced to get over whatever uneasiness lurked between them. They could hardly avoid each other forever.

She sighed and drew Little Bit to a halt while the rest of the group forged ahead. Maybe Alexis was right—assuming Tessa was correctly interpreting her motive. Maybe this trail ride was just what she and Cole needed to acknowledge the rift between them and, if not repair it, at least agree to let it be for the sake of their ministry.

She straightened her spine and lowered her heels, signaling to Little Bit that it was time for action—both for her and for her horse.

Cole wore his dark brown Stetson low over his forehead, but that didn't prevent her from seeing the scowl that furrowed his brow as he reined in beside her. His expression was as dark and sullen as she'd ever seen it. It was obvious he was struggling to get over his emotional hurdles. He just handled it differently than she did—with anger, apparently, or at least frustration.

He didn't used to be that way. He'd been a carefree young man who wore a smile on his face, a glint in his eyes and his heart on his sleeve.

They rode in silence for the first couple of miles, keeping to their own thoughts. Tessa pressed her despondency to the back of her mind and focused on relaxing her muscles, knowing Little Bit responded to whatever stress she was feeling.

With some difficulty, she shifted her concentration to the young people under her care. She knew better than to let her mind wander, especially on the first trail ride of the Mission Month, where an incident could emerge quite suddenly and require an immediate response. The horses were trustworthy even under duress. It was the teenagers she was worried about. At least one of the kids was likely to push the boundaries, and it was up to her and the other adults on the trail with them to catch the behavior early before someone got hurt.

Concentrate.

She was trying. Really she was. But Cole's very presence was an antagonist she couldn't ignore. What was the saying about acknowledging the elephant in the room? Or in this case, the one who was lumbering about on the large stretch of Texas ranch land, trumpeting its horn with loud abandon.

She chuckled at the mental picture her thought had created. Cole glanced her direction, arching his brows.

"What?" he asked, his voice low, coarse and cautious.

"It's nothing." She attempted to force a smile but missed the mark. It felt more like a grimace. "I was just thinking about something that struck me as humorous. Private joke."

Cole didn't press her and she didn't elaborate, but now that the ice had potentially broken between them, she saw the opportunity to fracture the unsettling silence in which they'd been riding. If they could maybe just speak to each other, carry on a normal conversation—even if it was as mere acquaintances or fellow employees—at least that would be something. Anything to get them moving in the right direction.

The only problem was, she couldn't think of anything to say, and Cole certainly wasn't attempting to contribute to the conversation. The silence stretched as tight as a high wire between them.

"Grayson is a real cutie-pie." Surely speaking about his son would be treading on safe ground. Everyone liked to talk about their children, right?

"Mmm-hmm." Not exactly the answer she'd hoped for. Actual English words would have been preferable. Elaborating beyond a mutter would have been nice.

"What is he now—eight weeks old?"

"Seven."

One word. In English. Progress.

"And I think you mentioned your father is watching him during your working hours here at the ranch?"

He nodded. Checkers surged forward suddenly, and Cole expertly reined him in. The horse shifted sideways toward Little Bit's flank. Tessa reacted instinctively and held her mount steady. Cole's Appaloosa's temperament had always been fiery and skittish. Apparently some things didn't change over time.

"I'm sure that's quite an adjustment for all of you. I think it's great that your dad wants to be so involved with the baby. Is Grayson sleeping through the night already? He seems so calm and sweet."

"Yeah, when *you* are holding him," Cole said drily and with more than a little punch. "Some evenings he goes right to sleep, but on others he's colicky and won't settle down. I've spent many evenings walking the hall for hours with the poor little guy, bouncing him and rocking and patting his back until his tummy feels better. You wouldn't believe the lungs on the kid. He could easily huff and puff and blow our house down."

"And it's all on you to care for him?"

Cole pressed his lips and jerked his chin affirmatively. "I try to give my dad the nights off, since he watches Grayson all day."

"You work all day, as well. That's a lot of responsibility on your shoulders. I don't know how you do it." She hesitated, wanting to ask the question that had been bothering her since she'd first discovered Cole was a single father. Now appeared to be the perfect opportunity, or at least as good as she was going to get. She understood that if a single woman got pregnant, she might sometimes be left to raise her baby on her own, but how did a single father end up in that position?

"If you don't mind my asking, where's Grayson's mother?"

Cole raised a brow. "Honestly? I don't know, and frankly, it doesn't matter much to me anymore. I've got full custody of Grayson, so I have no interaction with her. My lawyer will stay updated on her location in case I ever need medical information or anything on Grayson's behalf, but otherwise we have no contact whatsoever." He paused and frowned. "That wasn't my call to make. It's the way she wants it. From the very beginning, she never wanted anything to do with Grayson."

Tessa detected an edge of anger to his voice, and no wonder. Even back in high school, Cole had grand ideals of marriage and family. A mother who didn't want her baby? Tessa couldn't even imagine such a thing.

"She doesn't want to see her son at all? Ever?" She tried to keep the astonishment out of her voice but knew she failed. She didn't want to sound as if she was judging—even if privately she had to admit that she was.

"No. Nora—Grayson's biological mother— considered him a mistake. A burden she wanted nothing to do with. From the moment she learned she was pregnant with Grayson, she had every intention of giving him away for adoption. Or worse. I don't even like to think about what might have happened had I not stepped in. Thankfully, I found out she was pregnant with my child before she could make those kinds of decisions, and I talked her out of it. It wasn't easy. I've never fought for anything so hard in my life, and Nora isn't a big fan of mine right now. Probably won't ever be." He scoffed. "Grayson and I apparently got in the way of her fun. I hate that my son will grow up without his mother, but I think he's better off. I had a lawyer draw up papers and took custody of my son the moment he was born."

Bewilderment blanketed Tessa like a thick fog. On one hand, the idea that Cole had stepped up and taken responsibility as a father was beyond impressive, especially when the mother didn't want any custody rights at all. Tessa couldn't imagine too many men who would do such a thing, and it spoke to Cole's character that he didn't walk away from his obligation to his child when it would have been so simple to do. But not Cole. He was a sailor and a cowboy, and even before he'd joined the military, honor and duty were written in his heart. Of course he would never abandon his own flesh and blood.

This was also why the story confused her. Clearly there was no love lost between Cole and the baby's mother, and yet there had to have been a certain level of intimacy for Grayson to have been conceived in the first place. Cole wasn't the type of man to have a meaningless fling—or at least, he hadn't been. She realized just how little she knew about him now.

"That was very—" She hesitated as she searched for the right word. Gutsy? Loving? Strong? Amazing? "Courageous of you."

He blew out a breath and shook his head. "What it was, was stupid."

Her gaze swept over his face, taking in the deep lines stress had left in its wake. He shook his head, and his shoulders and arms tightened, his biceps twitching with strain.

Was he talking about the circumstances that had led to Grayson's birth? Surely he didn't regret taking custody of his son?

"Well, I think you've done a very loving thing." Though they'd parted on bad terms, Tessa knew Cole's capacity for caring about someone, and she knew beyond a doubt that he would give Grayson every bit of his heart. "God will bless you for your sacrifice."

Cole shook his head "That's what Alexis

said, and you both couldn't be more wrong. It's not a sacrifice. It just *is*. I don't walk away from my mistakes, or my obligations."

"No, I know you don't. That's not what I meant."

"That came out wrong. Grayson isn't a mistake. I never knew I could love a human being as much as I do that baby boy. It's just that I hate the…" His sentence skidded to a halt, and his jaw tightened.

The way it happened?

Cole had always fostered a deep faith in God in his heart. Whatever else had changed in his life, Tessa couldn't imagine his faith would have faltered. But he wouldn't be the first man—or woman, for that matter—to find himself succumbing to temptation. The only difference here was how Cole had responded once he found out his actions had had permanent repercussions. Her heart expanded at the thought.

Tessa looked away from Cole just long enough to glance up the line. One of the boys, Matt, had turned backward in the saddle and was making all kinds of ridiculous noises. Screeching, yelling, whooping and hollering it up—exactly the kind of thing that would send most horses bolting.

Crazy kid was trying to get the girls' attention, no doubt. Not thinking about what would happen if his horse decided to take off from underneath him. He'd land on his merry little bum, and then they would see who would be smiling and laughing. She didn't know whether to chuckle or shake her head. *It* was starting. The challenge of Mission Month was about to explode into full gear.

She searched for Marcus and found him up near the front of the line, enjoying Sissy's easy gait as he conversed with Alexis. It figured. He didn't spare a backward glance behind him, and he wasn't paying any attention to what was going on down the line. Probably figured she and Cole would pick up the slack—which, apparently, they were going to have to do.

"Hey!" she shouted to Matt, kicking Little Bit into a brisk trot. Normally she'd keep her own voice down, but in this instance, she wanted to make sure she was heard over the boy's earsplitting antics. "What do you think you're doing? Your horse is going to take off from underneath you. This isn't a carousel. Stop clowning around and turn back in your seat where you belong."

Matt merely laughed at her suggestion—at

least until his eyes met hers and he realized, probably from the scowl on her face, that she meant what she said. He griped loudly in protest but reluctantly turned forward in the saddle and stopped his screeching. Hotshot kids didn't think before they acted. It was a good thing for him the horses were all well vetted or he would have been in a world of hurt. Literally.

From her very first experience on a Mission Month, Tessa had learned that the young people would press their luck to see how much they could get away with, especially early on. Many of them were well-to-do and used to getting their own way. Fortunately, it usually didn't take long for them to realize Alexis and her team weren't kidding around. They were strong enough to deal with both foolishness and stubbornness and, ideally, to redirect the teenagers into more productive emotional expressions.

There was plenty of affection and kindness to go around, pouring from all who came into contact with the kids, but sometimes the *tough* had to be woven through the youths' lives before the sweet side of the love could truly be threaded in.

Today, Matt would be learning a hard lesson, starting with Tessa's scolding in front of his peers and ending with a very large stack of potatoes to peel when everyone else got time off.

"See me when we're finished with the trail ride. You've just earned yourself KP duty, mister, while your friends are going to be out enjoying the evening. They'll be playing games while you're chopping vegetables."

"Playing games? Like a bunch of little kids?" Matt gave her a silly smile that she imagined sent many females in his own age range into the clouds.

How annoying. Why did guys always think they could get away with things with a wink and a smile?

"Oh, come on, give me a break," he pleaded.

She wanted to roll her eyes, but instead she narrowed her gaze on him. "You want to push me and make it a week?"

Matt started to say something else and then seemed to think better of it. He shook his head and slumped in the saddle.

"Sit up straight or Ginger here won't know you're in charge."

This time he wisely did as he was told— *without* giving her any guff about it.

Better. She smiled, satisfied with today's

progress. They'd get where they needed to go with Matt. She was sure of it.

One kid down, eleven to go.

Marcus turned Sissy around and trotted toward her, examining the line of teenagers and horses as he went. *Now* he came to help? She snorted. Better late than never.

"We're all good back here?" he asked, flashing a smile that was curiously similar to Matt's earlier attempt at getting his way. And just about as effective.

"No thanks to you."

"So you had to play the old battle-ax, huh?"

"Ha! Keep talking to me that way and you'll find yourself on the sharp edge of a battle-ax, you jerk."

"Tessa," Cole called from behind her, his voice laced with raw concern. "One of the girls just took off in another direction. Should I bring her back in line?"

Tessa glanced over her shoulder. One of the teenagers, Briana, was, indeed, heading down a different trail, but it was immediately apparent to Tessa that it was the horse doing the leading and not the other way around. Unlike Matt, who'd made all kinds of noise, Briana's jaw was dropped in a silent scream. Her enormous eyes sparked with terror. She hoped Cole recognized the teenager's lack of control as well, and didn't try to mimic the kind of counseling she'd just given Matt. The last thing a panic-ridden, inexperienced rider needed would be anything that resembled the chewing out she'd just given Matt.

Fortunately, Cole had paired Briana up with Zephyr, who was one of the gentlest and most trustworthy horses in the stable. Just as his namesake indicated, he was a breeze to ride. He wasn't easily spooked and was well adapted to green riders. On the other hand, Briana must have somehow accidentally guided him the wrong direction. He and Briana were headed down an intermediate trail with a rather large embankment not more than twenty feet in front of them. It was a good obstacle for later on in the Mission Month when the teens were used to riding, but right now Tessa could think of nothing worse.

"Hurry, Cole. There's a—" she started, but it was already too late. Zephyr had nearly reached the two feet high edge. Poor Briana was clinging to the saddle horn like a lifeline, the horse's reins forgotten and dropped well over his neck.

Cole leaned forward and kicked his horse into a canter, but Zephyr reached the embankment before Cole did. Tentatively the horse stepped forward, his front feet reaching the landing below while his back hooves remained at the top of the rise.

And then Zephyr stopped.

Just...*stopped.*

Two hooves down and two hooves up, his flanks in the air and his long tail twitching back and forth.

Instead of clearing the embankment as Tessa expected him to do, Zephyr dropped his head and started grazing on the nearby grass, just as calm as you pleased. He didn't appear to notice the awkward position he was in—never mind that he still had a rider on his back. He seemed completely oblivious to the fact that a terrified human being still clung to his saddle.

Thankfully, Cole reached Briana's side. Tessa couldn't tell whether Cole's low tones were for Briana or for Zephyr as he reached for the horse's head and guided him the rest of the way down the step, but she breathed a sigh of relief when the horse was once again on flat, solid ground.

Crisis averted, thank the good Lord. Cole removed his Stetson, wiped his brow with the sleeve of his shirt and did the one thing Tessa never imagined he would do.

He laughed.

Cole had never seen anything like this horse's crazy antics in all his life, and he'd seen many things over the years. Whatever had possessed Zephyr to stop the way he had? Crazy equine.

He'd immediately recognized that the girl thought she was in distress, but it hadn't taken much to fix the problem. Clearly she was a new rider. Good for her for staying in the saddle. Thankfully he'd been able to guide the horse forward until Zephyr put his hind feet in league with his front ones. Now all Cole had to do was lead the errant horse and rider back to the rest of the group.

Problem solved.

He was in the midst of turning Zephyr around when the girl burst into a loud, agonizing wail that sent a chill skittering up Cole's spine.

What was her name again? Briana?

Why was she crying? If she wanted her horse to bolt out from under her, that sound would be just the ticket.

All was well that ended well, right? She was

safe enough now—and always had been, really, with Zephyr's level disposition and Cole right behind her. He ticked off other possibilities in his head. She'd managed to stay in the saddle, so she hadn't been physically injured. She might be freaked out some, poor girl, but surely she realized the worst of her traumatic experience was over.

Unless she kept up the sobbing, which was enough to shake up a grown man. He shuddered.

He pulled Checkers closer to Zephyr's side, hoping that would help Briana feel safer and more confident. Cole also wanted to make sure Zephyr kept his head, since clearly the girl had no idea how her voice and actions might affect her mount.

Marcus pulled up on his quarter horse and slid to the ground, then held up his arms to the still-sobbing youngster and grinned at her.

"Hey, now, little lady, let's get you back on your own two feet for a minute. Get some ground underneath you. Don't worry. Cole has your horse, and I've got you. Nothing bad is going to happen here."

The girl sniffed and ran her palms across her now-flaming cheeks and then allowed Marcus to help her dismount.

"There you go," Marcus said, holding her elbow until she gained her footing. "Steady now. See? It's all good. I've got you."

Briana had not only stopped crying, but she was now gazing up at Marcus as if he made the sun rise in the morning. Her hero.

Cole scoffed softly and bit his tongue to keep from adding his own remarks. Mr. Knight-in-Shining-Armor clearly didn't know the old adage about getting back up on a horse after being thrown from it.

Not that Cole had let Briana fall off the horse. Far from it. But he was certain the principle was the same. Briana needed to face down whatever mental obstacle it was that had tried to best her. He assumed the girl had been crying because she'd been frightened of Zephyr, or at the very least of the crazy horse's two-hoofed antics. The best way to get over her fear was to keep riding, to say nothing of the fact that she would *have* to ride in order to return to the homestead. They were too far out to walk back even if she'd wanted to. He could lead Zephyr if it made her feel more secure, but she'd still have to be in the saddle.

Alexis had halted the line of trail riders, and every eye was staring in his direction—or rather, at swoop-in-and-save-the-day Marcus and his charge. Had no one noticed that *he'd* actually done the saving?

Apparently not. The only one *not* looking at Marcus was Tessa, and her gaze was burning a hole clean through Cole.

It had been a long time since he'd spent any time with Tessa, and his interpretive skills might be a little rusty—not that they were ever that great to begin with—but she looked astounded. And if he didn't miss his guess, disappointed.

What had *he* done? He'd just saved the day, Marcus or no Marcus, but he wouldn't have known that from her expression.

Unfortunately, he couldn't exactly ask Tessa what she was thinking, since he was still holding Zephyr's lead rope.

"What are you planning to do here?" he asked Marcus, trying not to clench his jaw as he spoke. Cole was used to giving orders, not taking them, and it rubbed him wrong that Marcus had by default taken the lead in this situation—not to mention the credit.

Not that Cole wanted to be making any decisions where adolescent females with dicey emotions were concerned. Better he let Marcus take that job—but that didn't make it any easier to swallow. A man had his pride.

"What do you think, little lady? Are you ready to climb back on Zephyr for me?" Marcus asked Briana with an overexaggerated Texas accent that made Cole's ears ache. "Don't worry about a thing, darlin'. No one's going to let your horse get away from you again. I'll keep a tight grip on Zephyr's lead rope for the rest of the ride. You're in good hands."

Cole wondered if anyone noticed that *he* was the one who still held the lead and had Zephyr under control. Technically Briana was in *his* good hands.

Marcus smiled down at Briana in a way that made Cole want to grind his teeth or lose his lunch—or maybe both. Ridiculous, that's what it was. Using a winsome smile as a way to charm the girl into compliance and forget about all her problems. Getting her all googly-eyed and out of breath wasn't going to help her become a good horsewoman. What had happened to straight talking and straight shooting?

Maybe that didn't work with teenage girls. But he recalled one teenage girl who didn't need silly grins and goofy speeches to learn how to ride a horse.

Tessa had always had a good head on her

shoulders. He hadn't needed to play games with her. Not ever. Unlike Marcus, she was still direct and candid, wasn't she?

Or maybe not.

It was disconcerting to realize that he really didn't have a clue anymore. His whole world had turned up on end since coming back to Serendipity, and especially since finding out he'd be working with Tessa.

Reluctantly, he turned his attention back to the drama unfolding before him. Once Briana was back in the saddle, Marcus remounted and took Zephyr's lead from Cole, then brought the girl and her horse back to her place in the line, signaling Alexis that all was well and she could resume the ride.

Cole guided Checkers back in line with Tessa's horse, but she studiously avoided his gaze, and whatever conversation she'd been attempting with him earlier was shot clear out of the water. Obviously she had a problem with him—or, to be more specific, with something he'd done—but he didn't know what that was. Better to get it over with.

"Are you going to tell me what I did wrong or just leave me to guess?" He couldn't help it if his voice came out as a growl.

Her eyes snapped to his. "Are you serious right now?"

He shrugged. What did she want him to say? If he'd known what the problem was, he wouldn't have been asking her about it, now would he?

"You made Briana cry."

He'd *what*?

How did she figure *he* was responsible for that girl's tears?

Her eyebrows rose at the same moment her gaze flooded with…*something*. He didn't know what. Disappointment? Pity?

He cringed, wishing he was riding anywhere except next to her. Back in the day, she used to be able to read him like a book. She'd always known what he was thinking and feeling, sometimes before he did himself. He hoped that fact, at least, had altered, although the prospect looked bleak. He didn't want or need Tessa to interpret his emotions for him.

"Cole, you laughed at her."

"What? I did not. I—"

Oh, man. Tessa was right. He *had* laughed—not at Briana, of course. It was Zephyr's antics that had him chuckling. But Briana wouldn't have known that. Shame filled him. He wanted to kick himself. No matter that it wasn't intended. He'd gone and trampled on an innocent young lady's feelings. No wonder she'd beamed when Marcus had ridden up. At least the counselor had been kind, even if he was too dramatic for Cole's liking.

"I...was laughing at the horse, Red," he said, feeling as if he should explain. "Zephyr was front side down and back side up and just grazing away like nothing could bother him."

One corner of Tessa's mouth turned up—a little. Maybe. But he wasn't certain, and he wasn't much trusting his instincts right now.

"Yeah, I saw that, too," Tessa admitted. "But Briana didn't understand. She was probably a little worried about getting hurt, but I can guarantee you she was mainly terrified about taking a digger. To a teenage girl with a group of guys watching her—well, let's just say there aren't many things worse in the world than being unceremoniously planted in the dirt. Except maybe the most handsome older man on the ranch riding up and snickering at her."

He swallowed hard and tried to ignore what her words did to his suddenly fluttering stomach. "Hey, watch who you're calling old." His words were careless, but his emotions were not. He'd gone and inadvertently upset a teenage girl. He should have realized, paid more attention. "I hope I didn't hurt her feelings. I really blew it."

"You'll learn."

"I don't think so. I'm clearly not cut out for this, and I've proven that today. Alexis didn't know what she was asking when she hired me on to be a mentor."

Tessa's smile returned. "Oh, I think she did."

He shook his head. Everyone was wrong about him. He couldn't even figure out how to help a teenage girl out of a bind. And the kids were supposed to look up to him?

"There is one thing you can clarify for me," he said, trying to understand all the nuances of what had gone down today. "You gave that boy a good setting down. But when we interact with the girls, it's different, right? Because we can hurt their feelings?"

"I don't let the young ladies under my charge get away with anything, if that's what you mean. But yes, sometimes I take a different tack with them. Matt was goofing around, and he could have hurt himself. He thought he was a better rider than the rest of the group. And I'm sure he was trying to show off for the girls. But he'll get what's coming to him, in more ways than one. Thanks to you, part of his lesson will be a whole lot more effective than chopping vegetables."

"Thanks to me? What did I do?" Cole seemed to be asking that particular question a lot lately. He wasn't sure he wanted to hear the answer. He'd already had enough blame cast upon him for one day—even if he'd fully earned every bit of the weight. He hadn't done anything to Matt, though. He was certain of that much.

"Ginger."

Matt's horse? "What about her?"

"You could put a preschooler on her and she'd be the sweetest, most attentive mount you could possibly imagine. She instinctively knows the little ones are inexperienced. It's a beautiful thing to watch her compensate for their lack of competence and the innocence of their riding errors."

"But?" He didn't know where she was going with this. How would a gentle horse help or hinder Matt's attitude?

"But you just watch what she does when she gets a rider on her back who acts like he's too big for his boots."

"I don't get it."

"You will. Let's just say Matt may find

himself brushed up against a few bushes and trees as the day wears on. Ginger has a wicked sense of humor."

Despite everything that had happened and the weight Cole carried in his heart, he couldn't help but join Tessa's laughter. It was quite a picture, a horse getting back at her rider by bumping him into things.

Which reminded him—

"What should I do about Briana? To make it up to her, I mean. I don't want her to think I'm a spiteful man. I wasn't laughing at her, and I'm appalled to think that she might have thought that I was. I need to apologize and tell her I'm sorry."

Tessa shook her head. "Don't worry about it. I think Marcus charmed her right out of any distress she might have been feeling. I'm sure you've noticed his upbeat personality. He has a way with the teenagers, keeping them happy and smiling. Briana probably doesn't even remember what set her off into tears in the first place."

"Maybe not, but I still think I owe her an apology. I want her to know beyond the shadow of a doubt that I wasn't laughing at her."

"It's no problem. Really. I'll pull her aside

this evening and pass the explanation of your actions along for you."

"You don't think she needs to hear it from me?"

"Don't make a big deal out of it, okay? It's probably better that we just let it slide and move on. But I promise I'll mention your apology to her."

"Thanks, Red." Cole felt the weight of anxiety roll off his back, and not only because he knew Tessa would fix his problem for him. It was much more than that.

For the first time since he'd returned to Serendipity, he didn't feel tension turning his muscles into knots because he was around Tessa. In fact, riding beside her now, he felt almost comfortable, like pulling on the softness and scent of a familiar sweatshirt. He closed his eyes for a moment and breathed in, enjoying the smell of the Texas grassland and the comfort of the gentle rock of Checkers's gait.

He'd missed this. The landscape. The peace. Tessa.

"Oh, no." Tessa's strained voice broke in on Cole's tranquility and brought him to instant alertness.

"What? What's wrong?"

"It's Whitley."

He looked around, trying to figure out what had Tessa on edge. Another teenager making trouble? They couldn't just ride their horses and enjoy the beautiful Texas landscape?

"Who is—"

He didn't get to finish his question. Tessa spurred Little Bit into a canter and rode up the line. At first Cole couldn't see where she was going, but then he spotted the problem at about the same time Tessa reached Whitley.

After Zephyr's crazy antics earlier, Cole thought he'd seen everything, but this one was new. Whitley was clinging to her saddle, which had slid off to the side of the horse, threatening to swing underneath. It was a dangerous position for a rider to be in, especially an inexperienced one. He was amazed the girl hadn't rolled off the horse and into the dirt.

And once again, he was to blame. How could this be happening?

His muscles once again in knots, he nudged Checkers with the heels of his boots. When he reached Whitley's side, he jumped from the saddle and joined Tessa in helping Whitley dismount without injuring herself. Marcus held the horse's head while Tessa and Cole tag-teamed, Cole sweeping the girl safely to the ground while Tessa shoved the saddle up onto the horse's back and checked the cinch—the very cinch Cole had been responsible for tightening.

He didn't get it. He'd been saddling horses since he was in preschool. He knew about horses' proclivity to bloat their undersides to keep the cinch loose and had experienced every other trick in the book where mischievous equines were concerned. A loose cinch was a beginner's mistake, and one he knew he hadn't made.

He couldn't possibly have caused this accident, and yet…the evidence was right there in front of him. The knot had loosened enough for the saddle to slide, but not so much that it slipped under the horse. He offered up a quick thanks to God for watching out for the shaken teenager.

"Who did this?" Tessa demanded, shifting the saddle to the appropriate spot on the horse's back and meticulously tightening the cinch knot. The saddle wouldn't slide around this time. "Whitley? Tell me who's responsible for this stunt."

Whitley pinched her lips and remained silent, but Cole didn't miss her inadvertent glance toward a couple of the boys nearby.

Neither, apparently, did Tessa.

"Do you have something you want to say?" Cole challenged a smirking blond kid whose jeans probably cost more than Cole had made in a month in the navy. It didn't take a genius to see he was one of the instigators. The boy shrugged and shook his head.

"No? How about you?" he asked the kid's indigo-haired friend, who was looking equally satisfied with his antics. If Cole had anything to do with it, he would wipe the smirks from both of their faces. Never mind peeling potatoes. These two guys deserved a swift kick in their behinds.

But before he could say a thing, Tessa whirled on the lads, her face as white as a sheet. He would have expected her cheeks to be flushed, because she was clearly angry enough to spit nails.

"You," she said, pointing to the smug blond, "and you. I want you off your horses. Now."

Cole wondered if anyone else noticed that she was speaking through clenched teeth. He wouldn't want to be those boys right now. No matter what her peaked complexion hinted at, she was steaming-from-the-ears mad.

The boys slid from their saddles, and Cole moved to hold their horses' heads.

"What do you have to say for yourselves?"

she demanded, narrowing her eyes at the young men. She marched back and forth in front of them, her hands propped on her hips.

"We were just trying to have a little fun," the blond-haired kid mumbled, looking at the ground and kicking up dirt with the toe of his white sneaker.

"You think it's *fun* to put a girl in danger?" Tessa fumed. "Whitley could have been seriously hurt. She could have fallen or been trampled or worse. It's a good thing I saw her when I did or who knows what might have happened. Are you two the only ones responsible here?"

The blond kid remained silent, his gaze focused on his shoes. Indigo glanced at his friend and then at Tessa. He swallowed hard. "Yes, ma'am."

"Well, there's something. At least you're owning up to it. I appreciate your honesty. Now I want to know what you're going to do about it. Reparation is in order."

Neither of the boys spoke up. Cole cringed. Couldn't they see Tessa wasn't messing around with them? Did they have a death wish or something?

"Apparently I haven't made myself clear," she continued. "For starters, I want to hear you—*both* of you—apologize to Whitley. Right now. Like you mean it."

Whitley's face turned the shade of a ripe apple. Cole wasn't sure she appreciated the extra attention she was getting. Not this way.

The blond boy shrugged. "Sorry," he mumbled under his breath.

"Like you mean it," Tessa repeated sternly.

"Sorry," the blond said again. "Uh, Whitley. We didn't mean anything bad by it. Sorry if we scared you. I'm glad you didn't get hurt or anything."

The other boy nodded voraciously. "Yeah. Me, too. Sorry, Whitley."

"That's a decent start, young men, but unfortunately for you, it's not good enough." Tessa continued to march between the two boys, reminding Cole of his recruit division commander in navy boot camp. She had a sense of authority about her that permeated both her voice and the air around her. "Here at Redemption Ranch, we have a zero tolerance policy where violence is concerned, and this—"

She paused and worried her lower lip. Cole's fists clenched the leather reins he held beneath the horses' chins, not because the horses were giving him any trouble, but because it was all

he could do not to step in and take over for
Tessa. She appeared to be faltering, if only
for a moment. He'd led his fair share of men
in the navy and knew he would have no problem exhibiting a commanding presence that
would have those ill-behaved boys shaking in
their fancy sneakers.

He restrained himself only when he realized Tessa had everything under control—
her features were evenly schooled and the
boys were slump-shouldered and cowering.
He didn't know why, but for some reason, this
particular prank had rubbed Tessa the wrong
way and made her especially emotional. Cole
admired the way she'd stopped herself before
she'd gone overboard and said or done something she might later regret. Yes, the boys had
played a mean joke on Whitley, but Cole didn't
think it had been malicious, and everything
had turned out all right in the end. Thankfully,
Whitley hadn't been hurt, and though it had
taken the boys a while to admit their part in
the prank, they now appeared genuinely re-
pentant. From the expression on Tessa's face,
Cole guessed she must have been thinking
the same thing and come to the same conclusion he had.

"I don't want to see anything like this happen again. One more prank and you guys will be out of here, sporting fluorescent orange vests and picking up trash along the side of the highway. Are we clear?"

"Yes, ma'am," the boys said in unison. Cole bit back a smile. Tessa would have them marching a straight line yet. He had to admit it was impressive to watch her with her teenage charges.

"And just to make sure you understand the severity of your actions, you've earned extra stable duties. You'll both be mucking *all* of the stalls every morning for a week. Up at dawn, no excuses. The rest of your friends will enjoy a break from that particular chore, which I'm sure they'll appreciate. They'll probably want to thank you," she concluded with a wry smile.

Tessa certainly knew what she was doing, Cole thought as he assisted the boys back onto their mounts. She'd helped those kids—all of them—and had taught them an important lesson. He had no doubt they would be better off for it.

He was amazed to find he barely recognized the woman she'd become. He'd once known a shy girl whose only extroverted act was giving life to her characters on a theater stage. Now she was a leader, mentoring new groups of teenagers on a monthly basis, and that was no easy feat. Not something he ever wanted to do. Tessa had obviously learned a lot in college and in her work at Redemption Ranch. She cared—really put her whole heart into her work. He knew it, and the kids knew it. She made a genuine difference in the world.

Which gave him pause. Sure, he'd done his time in the navy. He'd do a respectable job as a wrangler here at the ranch. But what good had he done in the world?

Chapter Five

Tessa sighed and leaned back on her heels, pressing her palms into her thighs and stretching the small of her back. She'd been hunched over piles of sheet music for what felt like hours now, although in reality it had been more like forty-five minutes. She and Cole were meeting in another half an hour to go over their ideas for the teenagers' musical performance for the June BBQ, and so far she had nothing.

It didn't help that she was completely distracted. How could she not be, with Cole in the picture? She shook her head at her perceived weakness. She and Cole had talked very little during the past week, other than when she'd phoned him to set up an appointment to solidify their plans for the barbecue.

That had been one awkward and stilted conversation, with her stammering and stuttering and him answering every one of her questions with the fewest words possible.

She'd never felt so mixed up in her life. Up, down, sideways and backward—and it was all Cole's doing. That he could affect her that way annoyed her to no end. How could a man she hadn't seen in over a decade have the ability to rattle her so completely, making her equal parts flustered and giddy?

Yes, okay, they had a history together, but they had both matured. She was not the flighty young girl she'd been when she'd last seen Cole, and he was not the green youth who had left Serendipity to join the navy and see the world. She needed to get a handle on her emotions and she needed to do it now, before they—before *he*—started affecting the quality of her work. The young men and women currently residing at the ranch needed *all* of her attention, not a counselor whose head was too often in the clouds.

Cole was in her mind even when she was purposefully going out of her way to avoid him. She hoped no one else saw her confused behavior. She'd never before had the inclination to drop her girls with the wranglers when it was time for them to work with the animals and pick them up when they were finished, but now she was making excuses for why she needed to be elsewhere.

Simply put, she wasn't quite ready to face Cole again after her behavior during the trail ride. Here she was, trying to encourage him as a mentor to the teens, and then she'd gone all ballistic on the boys for their mean-spirited prank on poor, unsuspecting Whitley. Not exactly the best example of how to be a good counselor.

Maybe her father was right. Maybe she wasn't cut out to be a counselor at a ranch for delinquent teenagers—not that she would have made a good lawyer, as her father wanted. She'd picked on Cole for his handling of Briana, and yet when it came to those boys and their reckless prank, her own behavior and overreaction had left much to be desired.

At least Cole had unintentionally hurt Briana's feelings. She'd purposefully lined those boys up like a firing squad and gunned them down with her words—or at least that was how it felt to her in hindsight. She had lost control emotionally, and there was no excuse for that.

She sighed deeply and straightened the pile

of sheet music nearest to her. She'd confessed to God and asked forgiveness from the boys, which she hoped would be an important emotional, spiritual and communicative lesson for them, one that they could actually emulate in the future. She wasn't entirely in the wrong when she'd lectured the boys, and they still had to muck the stables for a week in reparation. Whitley could have been seriously hurt by their prank. But she still felt awful about the way it had gone down.

Music, she reminded herself, pulling out her cell phone to check the time and make sure there weren't any pressing messages or emails. Like from Cole, saying he wasn't going to show up. She half expected that's exactly what was going to happen. He'd made it clear he wasn't thrilled about having to participate in this project. But then again, neither was she.

She'd sorted through at least a hundred different pieces that the town kept in the small storeroom at the community center in a steel file cabinet so old the drawers barely opened. Most of the music pieces she'd sifted through were traditional Broadway tunes—the good stuff, where Tessa was concerned, but nothing that a group of modern urban youths would be interested in singing.

She might have been roped into this project against her will, but she hoped she would be able to catch the teenagers' interest with the program. There were quite a few country and Western pieces, but again, not anything that had been written in the past couple of decades. Anyway, country music reminded her of the day she'd broken up with Cole. She didn't even want to go there.

She blew out a breath and brushed a stray lock of hair back behind her ear.

"No luck finding anything yet?"

Cole's resonant voice startled her so completely that she fell backward, landing squarely on her bottom and sending piles of sheet music flying into the air.

He chuckled and bent to retrieve the papers nearest him, stacking them in a neat pile. "I hope these weren't in alphabetical order."

"Of course they weren't," she replied tartly. He reached for her and she reluctantly accepted his offer of assistance to right herself. *So much for dignity.* "I had them ordered by genre."

"My bad." His chuckle turned into a roll of laughter rumbling from deep in his chest. He took one of her hands in his and curved his other arm around her waist as she stood. He didn't look as if he was here against his will. In fact, he appeared to be in a good mood.

"Oh, you brought Grayson." She gestured toward the infant car seat, which Cole had evidently put down when he'd stooped to help her.

He flashed her a crooked grin. "I hope you don't mind that I brought him along with me. My dad's back is acting up again. I didn't want him to have to care for a baby when he's in pain, so I sent Dad to bed and ordered him to stay there. I just changed and fed Grayson, so he shouldn't be too much trouble."

"Of course I don't mind that you brought your son," Tessa exclaimed, reaching to pull the car seat nearer to her. "He won't be any trouble at all. I've been waiting for the opportunity to spend more time with this little guy."

The second the words were out of her mouth, Tessa wished she could take them back. Her face flooded with heat. She'd probably given *way* more thought than she should have to Grayson and his handsome father, but to have blurted out those feelings—how was Cole going to interpret *that* illuminating statement?

She backtracked the best she could. "I hope your dad feels better soon."

He cocked one eyebrow, and his blue eyes darkened to a stormy gray and filled with emotions Tessa couldn't even begin to name. He looked as if he was going to speak, but then he appeared to brush off whatever thought he'd been about to express. She didn't know whether to be relieved or curious about what he might have said. Perhaps both in equal measure. He turned his attention to his son, dropping forward onto his knees in order to be closer to Grayson's car seat and rocking it gently to keep the baby calm.

Tessa's chest tightened as she watched Cole with his infant. How could she not appreciate the love and gratitude pouring from his gaze, the smile on his lips that softened his features without taking away any of his masculinity? If anything, he'd never looked like more of a man than he did in his new role as a father. When he looked at Grayson, he lost the hard lines of stress that usually marked his face and the worry on his brow.

"So what are we going to do here?" he asked after a long pause. "About the music, I mean. What did you pick out for the kids to perform?"

"What did *I* pick out?" His question caught her by surprise, partially because her mind had been dwelling on him and his relationship with Grayson, and partially because she didn't know how he'd gotten the notion that she was in charge of selection. They were supposed to be collaborating on the project, and they still had ten minutes yet before they were even technically supposed to meet. And he thought she'd be ready with the music they were going to use? That she'd already made all the decisions?

His assumptions rattled her more than she cared to admit. "Actually, I'm a little overwhelmed by the choices. As you can see, there are hundreds of sheets of music in the file cabinet. I was hoping you'd have some ideas to contribute," she said, rustling another stack of music to a semblance of order. "I'll be honest. At this point I don't even know what genre I ought to be looking at."

He held his hands up, palms out, as if to stop her flow of words. The lines of strain on his features had returned. "I'm here because I know better than to try to talk Jo Spencer out of anything, but that's as far as it goes. This is your thing, Red. I don't want to get in your way. Whatever you think is best. I'll leave it entirely up to you."

She gaped at him, righteous indignation

and resentment swelling within her. Where had the pleasant man who'd greeted her only minutes earlier gone to hide? This was the guy who'd come back from the navy. Hardened and cynical.

"Are you serious right now? You're dropping the whole thing on me? We were *both* asked to do this."

He shrugged. "I don't know how I'm going to be able to help you. I'm not mentor material. And as for music and theater—really not my thing. I'm not a singer. I was into football, remember?"

Oh, yes, she remembered, all right. Despite how annoyed she was with the man, warmth filled her chest and her stomach fluttered with the memory. Cole had been a football player. One of the stars on his team. *She'd* been the theater geek, the senior female lead in the annual high school musical production.

And then Cole had—

Her gaze met his and she forgot to breathe. His eyes warmed and sparkled with emotion as their thoughts became one. His expression grew serious and his Adam's apple bobbed as he swallowed.

The world seemed to stop turning. The community center storage closet with its messy piles of sheet music littering the floor faded away.

They were there together in the past, deep into their shared memories.

The stage. The song. The gentle brush of his lips against hers.

He groaned softly. She thought it might have been her name. No—not her name. His special nickname for her. *Red.* He reached out a hand, drew his thumb along the base of her jaw. Framed her face, his fingers tangling in her hair. He leaned toward her, and she toward him. He angled his head, his warm breath fanning softly over her cheek. She closed her eyes.

And then Grayson wailed.

With an audible gasp, Tessa pulled away from Cole, her pulse roaring in her ears. What did she think she was doing? She felt dizzy and a little bit ill.

Cole scowled and turned to care for his son.

What had just happened—or almost happened?

For a moment, it had been as if the years had melted away, as if all the past hurts had never existed.

But they had. They did.

The feelings of loss and betrayal were all

real, and they came zipping back at her, inside her, sharp and aching.

Cole looked dazed, as if she'd just slapped him. He cleared his throat and reached to unstrap Grayson from his car seat, regaining his composure as he embraced his son.

"Shush now. It's okay, little man. Daddy's here."

Tessa scrambled to her feet, her head and her heart tumbling over each other. One second she'd been angry with him for dumping the whole project on her, and the next she'd nearly kissed him. What had she been thinking?

That was the problem. She hadn't been thinking at all. With the mere mention of their past, her mind had promptly meandered into a history that was beyond repair, even if she— if *they*—wanted to try. Talk about making things go from bad to worse.

They both seemed to know without speaking that they needed a moment to recover. While Cole fussed over Grayson, Tessa filed folders of sheet music in the battered metal cabinet. None of it was any use to her, anyway.

She watched Cole and Grayson out of the corner of her eye. She'd always known Cole would be a good father, but the emotional maturity he had displayed just now impressed her. He'd been able to shove what had happened between them aside in the blink of an eye in order to care for his son.

He really was a different man now, a man she didn't know. One who carried a heavy burden on his shoulders, yes, but also a man who could force those burdens aside for the sake of his child.

"What?" he asked when he glanced up and caught her staring at him.

"Nothing. I was just thinking about how the years have changed you—us," she corrected herself, heat flaming her cheeks. "You're an amazing father to Grayson."

He made a sound from the back of his throat that almost sounded like a growl. "I don't know that I agree with your assessment. I'm still on a tremendous learning curve where babies are concerned. Oftentimes I find myself feeling overwhelmed by all the responsibilities. I can't imagine how I would have handled it if—"

His sentence slammed to a halt, leaving dead air in its wake.

"If what?" she prodded softly, not certain she wanted to hear the answer. She suspected she knew how this was going to end.

He ran a palm across the stubble on his jaw. "If we— If you and I had gotten married. You know, right out of high school. I thought I had everything in my life figured out, but I certainly wasn't ready to be a father back then, even though in my ignorance I believed that I was. I'm not sure I'm ready for the challenge now, though I'm doing the best I can under the circumstances."

"Parenthood is something I don't think anyone is really ready for. Not that I can claim to be any kind of expert on the matter."

"No, but when I think back on what almost happened, I can't even fathom the consequences. We were just kids ourselves back then, not much older than those kids at the ranch. Can you imagine if we'd—"

"I don't think a Broadway musical number is going to work for this group of teenagers," she blurted, thrusting a random sheet of music at him. "I've considered dozens of them, but we're never going to catch their interest with 'Climb Ev'ry Mountain.'"

Cole looked perplexed for a moment, and then his gaze slowly turned to acknowledgment and acceptance.

"No. That's definitely not going to work."

"Suggestions?" She was relieved that he

was willing to change the subject. "I'm open to just about anything at this point."

"Hip-hop?"

"Absolutely not," she exclaimed. "I might have spoken in haste when I said I was open to anything. There will be no twerking at this barbecue."

"I don't even know what that is." He raised Grayson to his shoulder and gently patted his back.

"You cannot imagine how fortunate you are," she said, relief flooding through her. At least they were back on neutral ground. Their banter felt easier, more as it had been when they were younger. "Now, seriously, I've considered using something out of a more recent Broadway show, one the kids might be familiar with. Nothing raunchy, of course. Just something cute that the kids can get behind."

Anything but *Phantom*. She didn't say the thought aloud. She didn't have to. Neither one of them would want to go there, even for a second.

"What about a country song?" he asked and then winced. Talking Broadway musicals was hard enough, but a country music song for the June BBQ…that was the very recipe for disaster, at least for the two of them. No matter which way they scrambled, they were coming up on the sinking sand of their past relationship.

But they had to do something, make a decision on the music, and Cole was right. Country might be the way to go.

"I agree with you on that," she said. "And it might be our best and safest bet with these kids." This was about the teenagers, no matter how uncomfortable she and Cole felt. "The only problem is that I couldn't find any sheet music newer than the late seventies in here. Johnny Cash. Willie Nelson. John Denver."

"I like John Denver."

Tessa chuckled. "As do I."

She appreciated his attempt at levity. At least he was putting a little more effort into helping her now.

"What if we did something like Rascal Flatts?" he suggested. "Do any of the kids know how to play an instrument? They wouldn't all have to sing. Of course, it's not critical, since we have Samantha and Slade to play backup in a pinch, or we could just get backup tracks, but it might be a good idea to find out if any of the teens have special skills."

"I don't know if any of the teens play instruments, but it will be easy enough to find out. And we should be able to track down some sheet music online."

"Okay, that sounds like a reasonable plan." He sounded relieved. "I don't suppose you have a laptop available."

She laughed. "No. And even if I did, the community center doesn't have an internet connection."

"Cup O' Jo's, then. Come on. I'll drive." He strapped Grayson back in the car seat and toted him out to his dual-cab truck.

Tessa followed, her thoughts racing almost as fast as her heart. She was confused by all the up-and-down emotions she was experiencing, especially when they were popping as fast as a machine gun. One second Cole was telling her that the whole project was on her, and the next he was leading her to Cup O' Jo's, his suggestion commanding but not domineering. Although she didn't know much about how he'd served his time, she imagined he had been a good leader in the navy.

He had given up what was clearly a promising career for Grayson's sake. Tessa thought she might only be scratching the surface of the sacrifice Cole had truly made to be with his son, and all under questionable circumstances.

She was beyond curious, and yet she of all

people had no right to ask about the particulars. She would have to watch herself or else she'd be blurting out questions that would be uncomfortable for both of them.

Where Cole was concerned, her mouth often ran faster than her thoughts did, and even though she shouldn't be the one to probe Cole's personal life, she wasn't very good at doing what people expected of her. Just ask her father, who'd sent her off to college to get a law degree, only to discover she'd changed her major to psychology. To say he was disappointed was an understatement.

Despite the way certain people—Alexis and Jo, to be precise—had seen fit to throw them together, the Serendipity community at large would no doubt expect her to steer clear of Cole, and he of her.

Now they were about to enter the town hub.

Together. The opposite of what people would expect.

Cue the gossip mill.

Cole hung his hat on a nearby chair and slid behind one of the computers located along the back wall of Cup O' Jo's Café, setting Grayson's car seat on the floor next to him. The baby had slept on the way over to the café, but now he was awake, staring wide-eyed at Cole and noisily sucking his fist, which Cole knew was a precursor to the wailing that would commence if he didn't get Grayson a bottle sometime in the next sixty seconds.

"Would you mind?" Cole asked Tessa, gesturing to Grayson and then to the diaper bag. "It's going to take me a minute to get online and find the sheet music."

Jo Spencer came by, offering a carafe of fresh, hot coffee and a boisterous welcome that echoed throughout the café. Cole kept his eyes on the screen, refusing to look around and see how their friends and neighbors would be viewing this awkward situation. He dumped two sugar packets into the black liquid, stirred it with a spoon and took a long sip from his mug.

Belatedly, Tessa responded to his question.

"Of course I wouldn't mind loving on this little sweetheart." Tessa's smile and the genuinely delighted gleam in her emerald eyes left Cole in no doubt that she'd been waiting for him to ask.

"There's a bottle of formula in the side pocket of the diaper bag. I warmed it up before I left the house, so it should be fine for him now."

"He looks like he eats well," she said, laughing as Grayson grabbed her fingers and rooted for the bottle.

"Well and often," Cole replied, his throat tightening around his breath. Tessa was the very picture of the perfect mother cuddling the baby—his baby—in her arms. He swallowed hard to dislodge the feelings overwhelming him. Turning to the computer screen, he opened a browser, training his attention on the website address Tessa had given him. His emotions were riding far too close to the surface and way out of his comfort zone. He needed to keep his mind elsewhere. Anywhere except on Tessa. He was relieved when the site came up, and he rapidly typed the name of the song they'd decided on into the search engine.

"Just wait until Grayson is a teenager." Tessa's voice was sweet and soft. "I'll bet he'll eat you right out of house and home."

"I'll say. I've watched the boys at the ranch put away more than three times their weight in food."

"Comes from peeling a lot of potatoes."

He chuckled, but when he glanced over the top of the monitor, he realized she was not laughing with him. In fact, her lips were turned down—not in a frown, so much, but as if something had made her sad. And it didn't take much to guess what that was.

"You know, Red, those boys on the trail ride deserved exactly what they got," he said. "That was plain-out mean of them to loosen Whitley's horse's cinch that way, not to mention the fact that she could have been seriously hurt. Hard to believe they didn't even think about the possible consequences."

"In my experience, teenagers rarely think things through to their logical ends. They don't have a mature view of their own futures, much less anyone else's. I doubt the boys wanted to see Whitley physically injured, but they had every intention of humiliating her. They have absolutely no conception that their teasing might hurt Whitley ten times worse than if they slapped her in the face."

Cole narrowed his gaze on Tessa. She sounded as if she spoke from experience. But she'd been well liked in high school, at least in Serendipity. In fact, she'd been a novelty—a pretty new girl coming into her senior year with a class who'd virtually grown up together. She'd had guys falling all over themselves for a date with her.

Even him. *Especially* him. He'd done something downright crazy to get her attention. Something that was coming back to haunt him now with this whole musical number nonsense. Ironically enough, his actions back then had worked. He'd gotten the girl. For a time.

There he went again, drifting off into the past. He forced his mind away from those thoughts. Again.

"You really care about these teenagers, don't you?"

"I wouldn't be here if I didn't." She shook her head and sniffed. "I'd probably be living some miserable existence in an urban law firm if my dad had anything to say about it. I can't even imagine how awful that would be. I've never cared for city living. Give me Serendipity any day of the week."

"Right." He remembered the part about her dad pressuring her to attend college for prelaw. Tessa had never been keen on that idea. Counseling impressionable young ladies was much more up her alley. "So you went to college with the intention of fulfilling your father's wishes. I know the idea of that career didn't set well with you. But I'm curious. Why did you change your major to psychology?"

"Because I thought I could make a difference as a counselor."

"You *do* make a difference."

She raised Grayson to her shoulder to burp him and shifted her gaze somewhere over Cole's right shoulder. "Sometimes I do. Sometimes not so much."

He was confused. "Are we still talking about Whitley here?"

"Yes. And no. There was a reason I overreacted when the boys picked on her."

"What?"

"Not long ago, there was a girl I was counseling named Savannah. When she first came to one of our Mission Months, she was super quiet and introverted. She'd been convicted for possession of illegal drugs, and I think part of that was her way of avoiding all the bad stuff going down in her life. Everyone at the ranch teased her, boys and girls alike. But somewhere during the month, she earned their respect. She really turned herself around. I was so proud of her, almost as if she were my own daughter. I don't know. Maybe I got too close. My professors in college warned me about getting personal. But how could I not? Especially with Savannah. We shared a special bond. By the time the month ended I thought—I hoped—life would go better for her."

"It didn't?"

Tessa's gaze returned to his, and the pain in the glassy depths of her eyes would have knocked him down if he hadn't already been sitting. She was reliving the events as she shared them with him, and it was breaking her heart.

Without thinking, he reached out and brushed his fingers across the soft skin of her cheek, reassuring her with his touch. When her eyes widened, he immediately pulled back. The distance suddenly stretched between them like an impenetrable gap. He clasped his hands tightly in his lap.

"I try to check up on all my girls from time to time after they've left the ranch. Find out how they're faring. See if there's anything I can do for them. Most of the time the news is encouraging."

"And Savannah?"

"Not good. She got pregnant. I was stunned by the news. It must have happened right after she returned home."

It was as if a shiv had gouged Cole's heart. This story was hitting way too close to home, to the circumstances surrounding his own life in relation to how Grayson was conceived. It was difficult to sit and listen. But Tessa clearly needed to talk about her, so he encouraged her to continue.

"That's a shame. I'm sorry she's had it so tough."

"Savannah's own mother turned her out of the house when she found out."

"She threw her pregnant daughter out of her house?" Cole was appalled and angry. "That's awful. I can't imagine a mother who would be so callous and uncaring." Actually, he could. Nora, Grayson's mother, was such a woman. But this wasn't about him. "What did Savannah do?"

Tessa shook her head. A single tear rolled down her cheek and Cole couldn't help but reach for her once more. He brushed the tear away with the pad of his thumb, telling himself it was because her hands were full, holding his son. But really, there was so much more to it than that. His connection to Tessa went far beyond words. Her heart was breaking for this teenager Savannah, and because Tessa was hurting, so was Cole.

"The last I heard, she was living on the streets. I suspect perhaps she went back to using drugs. I don't know for sure. And I never heard what happened to the baby. It makes me sick just to think about it. I can hardly look at an infant now without—" She seemed to realize what she was about to say and paused, shaking her head. She pressed a slow, gentle kiss to Grayson's forehead.

"I'm so sorry," Cole said, but he knew his words were not nearly enough. Past or no past, he wanted to pull Tessa to her feet and wrap his arms around her, protect her from all the emotions she was drowning in. He probably would have acted on the urge, except she was holding Grayson, making an embrace less than ideal. Also, they were currently in the middle of the most public arena in Serendipity. There would be far too many curious stares and no stopping the gossip that would follow.

And anyway, who knew if she'd even accept his consolation? He could see she'd walked the plank in this teenager's place, shouldering the blame for what had happened to the young lady. And he could do nothing to change that or make it better for her. He wasn't good at using words, but he felt helpless to do any more than that.

"You couldn't possibly have predicted what was going to happen."

"No, I know that. In my head, I know. My heart is slow to follow. And it haunts me, the not knowing."

"I'm really sorry for that young lady, and I'll keep her in my prayers. That's not right, a mother tossing her daughter to the curb, especially when Savannah needed her the most. Parents ought to love their children despite their faults."

"I know, but Savannah's mother was never a great role model to her. In fact, I suspect that's where Savannah first got her drugs. From her mom. I don't think the woman was capable of being a real parent to her daughter."

"Savannah's father?"

"Out of the picture. Savannah never knew him."

"And the father of Savannah's baby? Where was he in all this?"

Tessa shrugged and Grayson gurgled in response. Her gaze dropped to the infant and she took a moment to console him. At length, she answered Cole's question, her voice a choked whisper. "Who knows where that young man got off to? He probably just didn't want to deal with the responsibility. It's easy enough for a man to walk away."

Cole nearly stood in surprise.

Tessa gasped and her eyes widened. "I'm so sorry. That was careless of me to say."

Cole wanted to punch a hole through the

wall, but not because of what Tessa had said. It was the thought of some kid getting Savannah pregnant and then just walking out on her, leaving her to deal with the *problem*. He just barely restrained himself from lashing out, and then only because Tessa was staring at him with a concerned expression.

He fisted one hand in the material of his shirt, low enough on his belly that Tessa couldn't see his response. The last thing he wanted to do was distress her any more, or Grayson, either, for that matter.

"This isn't a question of what's easy," Cole growled, trying and failing to keep his voice even. "That young man should be shot for walking away from his responsibilities."

Their gazes met and held.

"Not every man has your strength of character. Or your sense of honor."

Cole grit his teeth until his jaw ached. "There is nothing honorable about the way I've behaved."

"With Grayson, you mean? I beg to differ."

He leaned back in his chair and crossed his arms.

"Did you love her?" Her words came out as barely a whisper. "You wouldn't be the first man to sow his wild oats, and we all make mistakes. I'm not here to judge you."

He scowled. "Tessa, I got a woman pregnant in a one-night stand." He was ashamed to admit he had violated his own moral code, everything the good Lord and his mama had taught him.

"Oh." She looked stricken.

He didn't know how she'd imagined it had gone down between him and Grayson's mother, but she'd been giving him a great deal more credit than he deserved. Maybe now she would see the truth about him. He wouldn't blame her if she never wanted to talk to him again after this, but he was going to tell her the truth, even if it hurt.

"I didn't even know the woman's name. Not until much later—when I learned she was pregnant with my child."

Tessa gaped at him for a moment but then seemed to recover her wits. "I know I said it before, Cole, but it's worth repeating. I'm in no place to judge. I've made my own share of mistakes."

"Thank you for that. I hold myself accountable, and there is no excuse for my actions that night. I had too much to drink, and I blacked out. I don't really know all the details. What I do know is that I woke up in a stranger's bed. And then to make matters worse, I sneaked out of her apartment before she woke up. I just couldn't believe I'd done something so stupid." He paused. "But if it makes any difference to you, I'd never done anything like that before. Or since. There were…extenuating circumstances."

He didn't elaborate. He couldn't. The fact was that he had been on his first night of shore leave in a long while in one of his buddies' hometowns. He wasn't a regular drinker. His friends had insisted they go to a bar, and he'd accompanied them as the designated driver. Mostly he'd gone with them because he didn't want to be left all alone on the first Saturday night of June, the anniversary of the night he'd proposed to Tessa. The night she'd rejected him in front of the whole town. It was just too difficult. Too dark. Too many memories.

He'd been trying to escape those memories. But when they'd arrived at the bar his friends had picked out, he'd encountered something his heart and mind hadn't been ready for. The singing group playing that night was Tessa's favorite, the same one Cole had hired to surprise Tessa for his very public proposal.

To his everlasting shame, he had reached

for his first drink and didn't know when he'd stopped—only that somewhere along the way, he'd picked up a woman and ended up spending the night at her place.

And as a consequence, he'd become a father.

There was a big chunk of that story he wasn't willing to share with Tessa. Not now. Probably not ever.

"Did you have to resign from the navy because of Grayson?"

"Resign? No." He shook his head. "But it would have been complicated. I would have had to have found a permanent caregiver for him, maybe even sign over custody rights. I wasn't willing to do that. Had I remained enlisted, I knew I would have missed out on milestones. You know better than most how it feels to be a military kid, moving from place to place with no real sense of permanence. I couldn't do that to Grayson, or to myself, for that matter, especially since I didn't have his mother's support."

She eyed him for a moment, looking as if she wanted to speak, but then she closed her mouth and turned her gaze away.

"You were about to say something. What is it?"

"It's nothing, really. I was just thinking about the conversation we had about our relationship when we were teenagers. We were both self-centered and self-absorbed. Unable to see past our own wants and desires, our own little unrealistic, pie-in-the-sky world. How could we have known it was pure fantasy? Life is a far cry from the dreams we imagined."

She was right. He'd proposed to her without giving a second thought to how his enlistment would affect her and any children they might have had. He hadn't even been thinking about children, except in some abstract house-with-a-white-picket-fence-and-a-dog kind of way.

And Tessa?

He hadn't given her hopes and dreams the consideration they had deserved. He now realized he hadn't even known what she'd really wanted out of life. If they'd married right after high school, she might never have been able to attend college to get her psychology degree when there was always the possibility they'd have to move again as the navy dictated, and that was to say nothing of the difficulties she would have encountered trying to build any kind of career. No wonder she'd balked.

"I'm so appreciative of what military families sacrifice on our behalf," she said. "But I knew I didn't have it in me to be that noble."

He'd been thinking along those very same lines. Until Grayson came along, he hadn't realized what the men and women he served with were giving up for the sake of their country. He'd been a single man with relatively few ties. Many of his friends in the navy were married and had families waiting at the port for them.

"I feel like I should've cut my dad a little more slack," she continued. "I never really thought about how hard it must have been for him, raising a daughter single-handedly while his wife was deployed. It couldn't have been easy on him. He was practically a single father. And then after Mom died, he was."

"No, you're right. That couldn't have been easy."

"But hey, I turned out okay, right? Not a complete social misfit?"

"Well…" he teased, but then his heart grew heavy as his thoughts progressed to their logical conclusion. "Honestly, I have to admit that I've wondered about that. Worried about it, actually. A lot."

"What? That I'll end up in a loony bin?" Her tone was still mild and humorous.

"No. Although there is that." He winked at her, trying to lighten the moment, but his thoughts were weighty. "I mean about Grayson. Did I really do the right thing for him by keeping him with me?"

"I don't understand. How could keeping him with you not be right?"

"After all the shameful things I've done, God turned around and gave me an enormous blessing in Grayson. I don't deserve him. But tell me the truth, Tessa. Am I being selfish to want to be a father to him? Would he be better off had I allowed him to be adopted into a family with both a mother and a father?"

"No." Her answer was so quick and definitive that it relieved some of the burden he had been bearing alone until this moment. "He is exactly where he ought to be—with the father who loves him. You can't believe anything else, Cole. There is no one in the world who could possibly care for Grayson the way you do."

He slicked a hand over his hair, but it fell right back down over his forehead. "You're probably right. I'm psyching myself out, aren't I?"

"Of course I'm right. And yes, you are."

"I can't help but think about it sometimes.

I always thought I would do things in the right order. Have a wife before I had a kid. There are things a woman can give a child that a man never can. My mama taught me all kinds of things a man ought to learn from his mother—not that I always listened to her. But who is going to do that for Grayson?"

"You will, for starters. And others will pick up the slack. It is what it is, Cole. If Grayson's mother doesn't want custody, then she doesn't. I'll admit it's less common to find a single father in your position, but there are plenty of single mothers out there raising sons and daughters on their own, not only living but thriving. You've got a good heart. Grayson is fortunate to have you as his daddy. Grayson also has his aunts Vee and Mary to spoil him rotten. I hope you'll consider me your friend. I would be honored to be a part of Grayson's life. And," she said, nodding toward the front of the café, where Jo Spencer was vigorously welcoming new guests, "I think Grayson is going to have all the female attention he can handle in this town. He'll have mother figures galore. He'll probably get fat from all the cookies they'll feed him."

Cole smiled. That much was certainly true. Grayson was already popular around town, and Cole and his father had received more casseroles in the past week than they could eat in a month. There was no shortage of well-meaning neighbors in Serendipity.

But as for a mother figure—Cole couldn't help but see what was right in front of his eyes.

Tessa—holding Grayson in her arms as if he belonged there. In some way, Cole couldn't help but think that he did.

Chapter Six

Cole was looking at her funny, as if she'd sprouted horns or something.

"What's wrong?"

"I—uh—nothing. I—" he stammered, tunneling his fingers through his hair. "I've got to go."

"O-kay," she said, drawing out the word. What was with the sudden change in his demeanor? "What about the music? Did you find it on the website? Did we even decide on anything definitively?"

"I pulled up the song we were talking about using. I really don't care one way or another if you pick that or something else."

He reached for Grayson, practically snatching him away from her. Her shoulders tightened. It felt as if she'd done something to upset him, and she backpedaled in her thoughts, trying to figure out what that might have been.

"I thought we were working together on this." Surely he would stay and figure out the details of their project, even if he wouldn't share whatever else was bothering him.

He looked around as if he was ready to bolt. But she was not ready for him to leave yet. For the first time since Cole had returned to Serendipity, they'd made real progress, had a conversation that wasn't laden with all the tension of their previous exchanges. At least for a while, it had been better between them.

And now it was as if he'd closed down. Slammed his mask back into place. Withdrawn from her, and she didn't know why. The ache she'd been carrying around in her chest for years returned. Expanded.

"Look, I don't care what you do," he said, his voice distant. Chilled. "If you want me to pay for the downloads, just let me know how much and I'll rcimburse you."

"Cole, no one is asking you to pay for anything." Why would he even think that? She almost felt as if he was saying that just to take a jab at her. She knew her frustration was showing, but really, what did he expect? "This is work-related. We're supposed to be collaborating on the teens' performance. My ideas *and* your ideas."

The whole afternoon had turned around three hundred sixty degrees. They were right back where they'd started, only now Tessa was more stymied than ever.

They'd had a major breakthrough in their professional relationship on that trail ride. For a while there, she'd begun to think they might be able to work together comfortably, or at least call a truce.

Today things had been different between them. A big improvement.

Until it had started getting personal. She should have known better. She should have pulled back instead of delving forward into subjects that would be difficult for both of them. It was probably more uncomfortable for Cole than it had been for her. She'd been happy to get her feelings out in the open. Clearly the same couldn't be said of him.

"We have to have the music ready if we're going to get together with the teens and hash these things out. We've got only a little over a week to teach them the music and add any choreography to it."

"Fine. I'll tell you what. You text me when

and where you want to meet with the teenagers, and I'll be there."

"Fine," she echoed, trying not to succumb to the hurt. The anger. They were bickering like a couple of old hens, and if they weren't careful, they would start drawing interest from the people around them. Maybe they already were. She furtively glanced around her. Thankfully, none of the other patrons in Cup O' Jo's appeared to have overheard their little—what was it? A quarrel? Over what?

Cole buckled Grayson into his car seat and grabbed his hat from the back of the chair where he'd slung it. "Later, then."

"Right. Later." She breathed out heavily, giving in to the anger rising in her chest. She wasn't mad, exactly. It was more that she was indignant about the whole encounter. If he was trying to hurt her feelings on purpose, he was succeeding. She wasn't going to hold him back if he wanted to leave. Good riddance to him. If he didn't want to collaborate with her on this project with the teenagers, then so be it. She would do it herself. She hadn't needed his help before, and she didn't need it now.

Swallowing her disappointment, she slid around to the other side of the table and checked the computer monitor. It was going to be difficult for her to think about music right now. Or teenagers.

Or Cole.

She finished purchasing the music they'd discussed and downloaded it onto a flash drive. Though Cup O' Jo's offered a free printer for the customers' use, Tessa figured she'd rather print her copies at home. She was in no mood to be in public right now, especially not when she was on the verge of an emotional breakdown. Tears burned in her eyes, and she wasn't sure how long she could keep them from falling.

She didn't cry when she was hurt. She cried when she was angry. Right now she was hurt *and* angry—at Cole, yes, but mostly at herself.

How had she let Cole affect her this way? Wasn't she beyond this?

She was gathering her purse to leave when Jo plopped into the seat she'd vacated. Jo was smiling. She was always smiling. But concern and empathy poured from her gaze.

Tessa sighed and leaned back in her seat.

Perfect.

She really didn't want company right now, especially in the form of Jo Spencer. The woman was far too intuitive, and Tessa didn't want to talk about what was bothering her.

"I saw Cole leave," Jo said, never one to mince words. "He looked like he was in a bit of a hurry. Did something happen between the two of you?"

"Which something?" Tessa asked, frowning.

"That bad, huh? I've been praying for the two of you. I know it can't be easy, finding out that your present circumstances depend on working through your past."

Tessa gasped softly and shook her head. "We're not working through our past. We're just trying to figure out how to work together *now*."

"How's that going for you?" From anyone else, the question would have sounded cynical, but with Jo it was 100 percent heartfelt.

Tessa ran a hand over her hair, smoothing the inevitable frizz. "It's not. That project you and Alexis suggested we work on together? The musical number with the teenagers? That's not happening. He bowed out, and none too graciously at that."

"Ah, well. I was hoping, dear, for both of your sakes, that the endeavor would be a good thing. I saw your heads together after you first arrived and thought there might have been a breakthrough."

"So did I," Tessa admitted, swallowing the bile that rose in her throat. "We're both adults now. You'd think we could act like it, at least enough to work together without bickering like a couple of children."

"He certainly lit out of here like his tail was on fire."

"Right? And the weird thing is, up until that moment, we were getting along. We were collaborating. And then suddenly we weren't. He went from warm to cold in a matter of seconds, and I don't know why."

"Who can say what is what where a man's mind is concerned?" Jo said with a short laugh.

Tessa groaned. "Tell me about it."

"In Cole's defense, he's dealing with a lot right now. Finding out he was going to be a father. Taking custody of his son. Learning how to be a dad."

Tessa nodded. Jo was right. She couldn't really blame Cole for being a little short with her. Okay, maybe he'd been more than a little short. But he'd admitted to having long nights with Grayson. Tessa wasn't sure she'd hold up so well under the circumstances, working in the daytime and taking care of a baby at night.

"My advice to you, my dear, is to cut him some slack."

"I will. I'm not going to push him on the idea of working together on this project when it's clear he doesn't want to do it."

Jo's blue eyes brightened, and her curls bobbed as she shook her head. "That wasn't what I said, dear. Don't be so quick to be puttin' those thoughts in his mind. He wants to work with you. He just doesn't know it yet. Men sometimes have to take the long way around workin' stuff out in their heads. Give him some time—and space—and just see if he don't come chasin' after you."

Tessa didn't want Cole chasing after her. She just wanted him to do his job and help her plan the program. Didn't she?

"Promise me you won't give up on the man," Jo urged, reaching across the table to squeeze Tessa's elbow.

Tessa sighed. She didn't know what difference it would make whether or not she gave up on Cole, since he had clearly given up on her. No—more than that. He was antagonistic toward her. Maybe not always, but enough for her to get the message, loud and clear. Nothing she said or did was going to change how he felt about her. She didn't have Jo's confidence that Cole would capitulate on the musical project, or anything else, for that matter. But she had few other options at the moment, and Jo was waiting for her response.

She took a deep breath and plunged in. "Okay, Jo. If you say so. I promise you I won't give up on Cole."

Jo nodded vigorously, her smile beaming like the morning sunshine. "I'm happy to hear it, dear. Happy to hear it. 'Cause God's got a lot in store for the two of you. Mark my words. You just see if He doesn't."

Nothing helped Cole's nerves calm down quite like a long ride on Checkers. Something about being in the saddle, enjoying the familiar, soothing rock and sway of his horse's canter, the fresh air and the sweet swishing sound of Checkers's hooves against the Texas prairie settled his soul in a way few other things did.

Gave him time to reflect. Figure out his next move.

Only today, tranquility eluded him. The harder he chased peace, the farther away it seemed.

Since he'd returned to Serendipity, it seemed as if every time he turned around, he was stepping into quicksand. His head and his heart were sinking fast, and the more he struggled, the worse it became.

He was man enough to admit he owed Tessa an apology, if not an explanation, for the way he'd stormed off. She hadn't deserved the cold shoulder he'd given her, especially after the conversation they'd had. They weren't teenagers anymore, and he'd acted like an immature idiot.

But maybe that was the whole point. They *weren't* youngsters. Time, life and experience had chipped away at them both, molding them into the people they were now. A man and a woman who were mere shadows of the youngsters they once were.

When he'd seen Tessa cuddling Grayson in the crook of her arm, as sweet and natural a mother as there'd ever been, he'd panicked. The past and the present had collided like a train wreck. He'd remembered how desperately he'd wanted to have a family with Tessa, even if it had been in his immaturity, and that had segued into—what?

He supposed it was the fact that they couldn't go back, and it wasn't as if they could move forward with any kind of personal relationship. At this point he was questioning the wisdom of trying to maintain a professional one.

They couldn't even be in the same room with each other without something happening, some thought or memory popping up out of nowhere and exploding around them. He was walking through an emotional minefield. He'd almost kissed her!

The best thing he could do was to shove all those feelings deep inside and do whatever was necessary to make his transition back to Serendipity a success, if not for his own sanity, then at least for Grayson's sake. The baby didn't deserve a father who became distracted every time a certain redhead walked by. If his job involved working with Tessa, so be it. He needed to deal.

He had enough on his plate adjusting to this new position at Redemption Ranch—this whole mentoring business and working with the teenagers. He couldn't imagine how anyone could come to the conclusion that he'd be a good example for impressionable kids, but Alexis and Griff had. And Tessa had.

He'd done nothing to earn that trust. If anything, he'd botched every mentoring opportunity he'd been given. Maybe the loose cinch hadn't been his fault, but the part with Briana had been a complete and unmitigated disaster on his part. He had made a bad thing worse. He hadn't handled that crying girl very well.

Handled it? He'd *caused* it.

Alexis ought to have fired him right on the spot. Instead, he was still mentoring the teens, directing a music number, no less. No wonder he'd balked like a skittish colt. Working on music with Tessa was out of his comfort zone on so many levels that he couldn't even count them.

Why should that matter? None of the officers he'd worked under in the navy ever paused to consider whether or not the orders they gave him fell out of his comfort zone. An order was an order.

This was no different. It was his job, end of subject.

He leaned forward, nudging Checkers into a gallop, letting the wind in his face ease the stress off his shoulders. He rode at a full gallop for about ten minutes and then turned back toward the Haddons' stable and allowed Checkers to maintain an easier pace. Cole's mind was blessedly neutral after the unnerving way it had been revving earlier. It was amazing what a good horseback ride could do for a cowboy.

He was looking forward to the day Grayson was old enough to climb onto the back of a horse. What a blessing it would be to have the opportunity to teach his son how to ride the way his father had taught him when he was knee-high to a grasshopper.

He was lost in happy thoughts when suddenly Checkers reared up underneath him. His horse had always been a little high-strung, so while the movement caught Cole by surprise, it didn't unseat him. He'd been riding this horse for so long, it was as if Checkers was an extension of him. He felt the horse quiver underneath him and realized something was…off.

He reined in, turning Checkers in a tight circle to calm him down and scout out the area around him.

And then he heard it—the sound that no doubt was the cause of Checkers' sudden flare-up.

The echo of weeping. A woman's high, distressed voice reverberated softly across the plains.

Cole tuned his ears to the sound, but he couldn't quite pinpoint it. He scanned the distance all around him but didn't see anyone, or any movement in the brush.

"Hello?" he called loud enough for the woman to hear him, praying that he didn't startle or frighten her. She'd caught Checkers off guard, not to mention Cole, so he suspected she probably didn't know he was there.

The sobs stopped abruptly, but the woman didn't immediately disclose her location. Cole waited, his pulse roaring through his veins as he realized he'd spoken before thinking the situation all the way through. The woman was out in the middle of a field a good half mile from the ranch.

She probably didn't wish to be disturbed.

Another thought struck him right on the tail end of the first, and it was twice as frightening.

What if it wasn't a woman at all? What if, instead, it was one of Tessa's teenage girls?

He groaned softly and removed his hat, wiping the sweat from his suddenly sticky brow with the sleeve of his shirt. He had the sudden urge to kick Checkers into a gallop and skedaddle right out of there, but he'd already announced himself to the woman. She'd heard his voice. And he could hardly ride away from a woman in jeopardy, whatever her age.

"Hello?" he called again.

He waited, but still no answer.

"It's Cole Bishop. One of the—er—wranglers at Redemption Ranch." His throat closed around his breath, and he had to consciously work to get air into his lungs. He'd stumbled over the word *wrangler* because another noun had popped up out of nowhere and almost forced itself into its place.

Mentor.

No doubt about it—he was going to regret this. He dismounted and left Checkers to graze, knowing the horse would stay within whistling range. He turned in the direction he thought he'd heard the crying coming from and cautiously stepped forward.

"I don't mean to intrude on a private moment," he said, trying to speak conversationally and holding up both arms in a goodwill gesture. He couldn't see her, but that didn't necessarily mean she didn't see him. He was quaking on the inside. He hoped his voice wasn't quivering. Or his hands. "I just want to make sure you're okay."

There was a rustling in the tall, dry grass a few feet in front of him as a young lady stood. Sure enough, he immediately recognized the girl as one of Tessa's from the ranch. Her eyes were red and swollen, and she didn't quite meet his gaze.

What was her name? Katie?

No—*Kaylie*. That was it.

"Hey, Kaylie. I'm Cole. Do you remember me from the trail ride?" He searched for the best way to broach the subject of why she was out in a field by herself. He figured he'd best steer clear of the emotional aspect of the equation, at least for now. "This is quite a ways from the ranch. Did you walk out here?"

Staring at her feet, she nodded in response to his question and brushed her long blond hair back behind her ears. She looked positively miserable, gnawing on her bottom lip and wringing her hands together in front of her.

Okay, now what?

Cole's thoughts roared, his pulse pummeling as he searched through his options. He knew his next words were paramount, the difference between her taking him into her confidence or turning and running in the opposite direction. He had a history of the latter where women were concerned.

The problem was, he didn't know what words he should say or how to console her. According to Alexis and Tessa, he was supposed to be a mentor, a guide for the young people, but look how that had turned out for him so far.

Not well. Not well at all.

Whatever was bothering Kaylie, it seemed like a pretty big deal, but what did he know about it? Teenage girls were all about drama, right? Getting emotional and blowing every little thing out of proportion? Maybe it was nothing. Then again, it could be serious.

What would a mentor do?

What would *Tessa* do?

"I—er—" he stammered, removing his hat and tunneling his fingers through his hair. He cleared his throat and tried again. "Is there something I can do to help you? Do you want to talk about…whatever's bothering you?"

The sound that emerged from Kaylie sent a shiver down Cole's spine. It sounded as if someone was strangling a swine. She crumpled to the ground and covered her face with her hands.

Cole's gut turned over as he dropped to his knees beside her, supporting her shoulders as she sobbed and patting her awkwardly on the back. He'd never in his life been quite so far out of his comfort zone as he was at this moment.

"Are you hurt? Do you need a doctor?" His

suggestion was just a wild stab in the dark, but she immediately began to wail louder, which made him suspect something he'd said had hit the target.

She didn't appear to be injured, and her distress seemed more emotional than physical. He pressed the back of his hand to her forehead to check for a fever. Her face was flushed, but she didn't feel warm. Her skin was clammy and cold.

"Why don't you come back with me? I'll take you to the Redemption Ranch homestead on my horse. Tessa will be able to help you better than I'm able to, and we can call Dr. Delia to come take a look at you, if you'd like."

"No!" Kaylie scrambled backward on all fours. "No doctor. Please. No doctor."

He held up his hands in surrender.

"Kaylie," he said, struggling to keep the frustration he was feeling out of his voice. He was quickly running out of options with her. "I won't call Delia if you don't want me to, but you've got to talk to me. I can't help you if you won't tell me what's bothering you."

She stared at him for a moment, clearly taking his measure. He steadily held her gaze, keeping his breath slow and even, praying the anxious teenager would see him as someone she could trust—at least until he could get her back to Tessa and Alexis. Surely they'd know what to do with the poor distressed girl.

"Promise me you won't tell anyone." Kaylie dabbed at her wet cheeks with her palms. She sat back in the grass and crossed her legs.

Tell anyone? What—some kind of secret?

If that was the case, then she probably wasn't hurt, at least physically. So why had she balked when he'd brought up the idea of seeing a doctor? Or maybe he was the one overreacting.

Maybe it was just some silly teenage girl freak-out-because-the-world-was-ending, bad-hair-day moment, after all.

"Sure. I promise."

Seemed simple enough. He wanted her to trust him, after all. He was working off the assumption that he'd been the one to find her out here for a reason, and not Tessa or Alexis, whom Cole imagined would have been much better candidates for this job. God must have His reasons, though Cole couldn't even begin to fathom what they were.

Kaylie cleared her throat and her gaze dropped to her hands, which she clenched and unclenched in her lap. Cole prepared himself to hear a dramatic sob story about a boy she liked not liking her back or some such teenage dilemma.

"I'm pregnant."

Cole was glad he was still on his knees with his palms braced against his thighs or he would have fallen over. As it was, his breath left him in a whoosh as if he'd been sucker punched.

In a way, he had been sideswiped—but not nearly as much as this poor girl had obviously been.

"Pregnant?" he repeated, his voice lower and tighter than usual. With the way his throat closed around his words, it was amazing that he could say anything at all.

"Seven months."

Seven months?

He caught himself gaping at her before he snapped his jaw shut tight. He didn't want her to feel any worse than she already did, but he couldn't ignore the shockwaves bolting through him. Somewhere in the back of his mind, he knew that as a mentor, he should be responding in a more practical and compassionate manner, but *seven months*?

He hadn't paid that much attention to her when he'd worked with her in the stable, so now he took a moment to examine her carefully, imagining he must have missed the obvious signs of her pregnancy—like the fact that she ought to have a protruding midsection. But she didn't. He couldn't discern a baby bump at all. The teenager was reed-thin, like one of those supermodels who survived on nothing but kale smoothies.

Granted, he didn't know the first thing about having babies. Grayson's mother hadn't allowed him to be part of her life at all until after the baby was born. But he did remember his sister-in-law Mary being the size of a house during her last months of pregnancy. How could this tiny wisp of a girl be so far along and yet somehow have hidden it from everyone? How had no one noticed? He wasn't the most observant of men, obviously, but Kaylie had been living in a bunkhouse with Tessa and five other girls for three weeks already. How did she keep a secret like that?

He casually returned his gaze to her belly, trying to examine her without making her more uncomfortable than she already was. It was bad enough that *he'd* been the one to come upon her in her distress. She didn't need some strange cowboy gawking at her and asking her a bunch of private questions about her pregnancy—like how far along she was.

Either she wasn't showing yet or else she was good at hiding it.

Talk about awkward.

He needed to call in reinforcements—immediately. Tessa, Alexis and Dr. Delia, for starters. He didn't want to be responsible for making this situation into more of a mess than it already was. The girl needed counseling—from a woman. It was high time to take Kaylie back to the ranch and help the poor child get the assistance she needed to make it through this crisis.

Tessa would know what to say, what to do, how to act in order to console the teenager. She would—

Oh, no.

He'd made a hasty and irreparable mistake. Before Kaylie had said a word about her pregnancy, she'd exacted a very specific promise out of him.

What an idiot he was. He'd agreed to her conditions without even pausing to consider the possible ramifications. He'd expressly said he wouldn't speak a word of what she'd just told him.

Which left him—*where?*

How was he supposed to help her if he couldn't bring Tessa in for backup? What was he going to do if he had to handle this situation all by himself?

He shifted into a seated position and leaned back on his hands, digging his fists into the dry grass. He knew instinctively that this was another make-it-or-break-it moment. If he said or did the wrong thing now, he might send Kaylie running a lot farther away than the half a mile she'd walked to get out into this field. She might disappear completely, and then there would be no one to help her.

His mind flashed back to the story Tessa had told him about Savannah, pregnant and alone on the streets. Cole couldn't let this tiny teenager with a loosely draped shirt that somehow completely masked her late-stage pregnancy end up as another statistic, as another Savannah with no place to go and no one to support her.

"Have you spoken to Tessa about this? Or Alexis?" He knew she hadn't, because Tessa and Alexis would have been doing all they could to assist her. His question was more to put the suggestion into Kaylie's mind—where she could turn for help.

"No!" Kaylie exclaimed in horror, bursting into a fresh bout of tears. Apparently she'd already thought about informing them and had rejected the notion. "You *can't* tell them. You can't." She reached for his arm and clung to it. "You *can't*. You promised."

"I won't say anything," he assured her, his voice grave. "But I really think you should. Tessa is the smartest, most compassionate woman I've ever met. She will know how best to help you and your baby. You can trust her. I do."

It was true that he had faith in Tessa as an outstanding counselor to these teenagers. She excelled at her job, and she would know what Kaylie needed to do. But he also knew he'd be placing Tessa in an emotionally traumatic situation that he wasn't certain she was capable of handling.

If Savannah's tragic story had immediately thrust itself into the forefront of his mind, how much more would it haunt Tessa's?

And yet Cole knew in his heart that's what Tessa would want him to do—lead Kaylie in her direction so she would have another chance to do whatever she could to help a troubled teenager.

Which left him in a quandary of epic proportions. He could see no way out of it.

He'd given his word to Kaylie, and to a man like Cole, his word was his bond. He'd vowed to remain silent concerning what she'd told him. But what if, by not speaking up and informing Tessa and Alexis of the situation, Kaylie ended up in worse circumstances than she already was? *Someone* needed to assist her, and he wasn't even remotely qualified for the task.

He had to help her—somehow. He needed more information. Clearly, her stay at Redemption Ranch was causing her no small amount of distress, and he could well imagine why, as she was trying to hide the truth about being pregnant when she was rarely if ever alone. But here at the ranch, she still had Tessa's guidance. What kind of support system would she have back home? Would she, like Savannah, be thrown out of her parents' house to try to make it on her own?

Again, his thoughts drifted back to the story Tessa had related to him. No girl deserved the bitter life Savannah must be living, no matter what kind of mistakes she'd made. And neither did Kaylie.

Cole could relate—more than he wanted to be able to. He was the poster child in the *life-changing mistakes* department where unplanned pregnancies and babies were concerned. He thought about sharing his own story with her but didn't know whether it would help matters or make them worse.

Tessa would know what he should do. But alone, without her guidance, he didn't have a clue, and he didn't want to make a serious error in judgment, so he kept his past to himself as he struggled through deciding what he should do next.

Tell Tessa? Not tell her and keep it to himself?

Was it ever okay to break a promise? What if his silence put Kaylie and her baby more at risk?

"What about the baby's father?" he asked, trying to discern what kind of support system Kaylie was looking at once she returned home. "Does he want to be involved?" Cole cringed inwardly at the neutral wording. But as much as Cole hated it, it was an unfortunate reality—a man could choose whether or not to be a parent to his child, and he could walk away and not look back, if that's what he wanted.

Kaylie snorted, and for a moment her gaze flooded with as much anger as there was anguish. "My baby's father is in college. I met him when he came to our house for dinner. Dad is a philosophy professor, and he loves to have his students over to debate issues. Dad said I couldn't date any of those college guys because I'm too young, but I snuck out and met with Thomas." She paused, and a sob hiccuped from her throat. "I thought he loved me."

Anger tore through Cole and he clenched his fists even harder into the ground, welcoming the distraction of the dry grass scratching his wrists. He could just imagine what that young man *thought*. And it had nothing whatsoever to do with love.

He took a deep breath and, with great effort, set the issue of Thomas's irresponsibility aside for the moment. Kaylie had failed to mention someone important, and he suspected that might be part of her problem. "What about your mother?"

Kaylie's weeping intensified. "She and Dad got divorced when I was little. I don't even remember what she looks like, except in pictures. My dad told me she doesn't want to see me. Ever."

Cole was floored, struggling to tamp back his own emotions as her story continued to hit closer and closer to home. Was Kaylie acting out because she didn't have a mother's guidance in her life? And if that were true, what would that mean for Grayson?

But now was not the time to question the wisdom of his own actions.

"This young man—Thomas. He knows about the baby?"

Kaylie pinched her lips. "I texted him and told him I was pregnant. He said he's not the father, that he wants nothing to do with me or the baby."

Cole had to bite his lip to keep from commenting on what she'd said. Only in this day and age would a kid send information as important as telling a young man he was going to be a father through a text message. Texting was too impersonal—and so much easier to simply ignore and hope it would go away. That's not how it would be if Cole got in this kid's face. He was already imagining what he'd do to the irresponsible young man. First he'd grab him by the collar and then—

"Thomas *is* the father," Kaylie repeated, her voice shaky but resolute. "He's the only guy I've ever—" Her sentence skidded to an awkward halt as heat suffused her face. "I thought we were in love," she concluded miserably. She shivered despite the heat of the day.

"I'm sorry for that. Men can be real jerks

sometimes. I know things don't always work out the way we'd like them to, and this whole thing might seem impossible to you right now, but I believe God has our backs, even during the worst of it."

"Yeah?" She sounded as if she desperately wanted to believe Cole's words.

"Yes. God's gotten me through more than a few moments like these in my own life. I know He'll do the same for you."

"Maybe," Kaylie conceded. "I'd never been to church, at least not until I came to Redemption Ranch. I'm still learning about God. I'd like that to be true, though—to believe that there's Someone up there looking out for me. That's what Tessa says."

Cole tried to force a smile through the tension coursing through him. "She's right. You should listen to her. She explains things a lot better than I do. And please—I hope you'll at least consider talking to her about all this. I know I've already said this, but I truly believe she can help you."

Kaylie shook her head vehemently and seemed to withdraw into herself, and Cole wondered if by his suggestion he'd just undone what little good he'd been able to do for her.

He might have broken that thin line of trust forming between them.

"At least let me take you back to the ranch," he insisted. He still wasn't clear on what he should or could do for her, but the one thing he *did* know was that Kaylie shouldn't have been wandering about the ranch on her own. She could have gotten lost, or injured, or bitten by a rattlesnake. "You can ride Checkers. I'll lead."

She nodded and allowed him to help her onto the back of the horse.

"Why do you call him Checkers?" she asked as he adjusted the stirrups to fit the length of her legs. "Those are spots on his back, not squares."

Cole chuckled, though it didn't reach his aching heart. "Checkers is short for Spot Check. It's a military term."

"You were in the military?" She sniffled and wiped her wet cheek with the back of her hand.

"Navy," he answered, pulling the reins over Checkers's ears. "Although I've had Checkers for longer than that. Since I was in high school, actually."

In one way, he was relieved that the conversation had segued into something less personal, but at the same time, he felt as if maybe he ought to continue pressing Kaylie for every last bit of useful information he could, not that anything he might learn at this point would help him assist her in any way.

The hard truth was, no amount of information was going to do him any good. Not unless he could somehow find the answer to the one question that kept echoing repeatedly in his mind—

What would Tessa do?

Chapter Seven

That Friday, Tessa led the teenagers into the community center to practice the music for the June BBQ. The actual performance would take place on a similar platform built on the town green, but for now, Tessa wanted to keep their rehearsals out of the public eye. It was supposed to be a surprise performance. She didn't want to give away their secret too early.

After much prayer, she'd wrapped her mind around facilitating the teenagers' musical number herself, and although she knew she would be wrestling with a number of old memories, she imagined the exercise would be good for the young people, giving them the opportunity to work together on something positive. Most of them didn't have that in their lives, didn't have close families who supported and guided them. That was often why they got into trouble in the first place. In the case of some of the kids who came from the well-to-do homes, they were given nearly everything in their lives without any work on their part at all, and with those advantages came a misplaced sense of entitlement.

They wouldn't find that here. This production was just for fun and they'd benefit from a welcoming audience, but they'd have to practice and earn the community praise she knew would be forthcoming. No matter what backgrounds they might have come from, Tessa treated every one of them with the same love and respect.

She had arranged six microphone stands across the front of the stage, imagining she could split the young people into couples and work out whatever manner of choreography she could manage to coax from them. She didn't have high hopes on that one. It was all she was going to be able to do to get them to sing, never mind put dance steps to the music.

At least the girls all knew and appeared to appreciate her choice of a popular country song. She didn't know a thing about the guys' taste in music, but she assumed it probably wasn't too different from the girls'.

"All right, everyone, let's line up here in the front, please," she called, pointing across the stage. "Those stands you see in front of you will have live microphones on them the day of the performance, so I'm going to pair you all up, a girl and a boy on each mic."

The girls giggled. The guys catcalled.

This would certainly be easier if Cole was around to lend a hand, but Tessa had no expectations of him showing up anytime soon.

"And just so you know, I'll be teaching you a simple dance to go along with the song."

Her announcement was followed with some not entirely unexpected groans, mostly from the boys. Five of the girls were huddled together, probably whispering about which boy they wanted to be paired with. Kaylie was included as part of that group but was unusually quiet, staring off into the distance instead of gossiping with the other girls. That gave Tessa pause, but at the moment she was far more concerned with poor Whitley, who stood apart from all of the other kids, her arms tightly wrapped around her middle and her chin tucked close to her chest. Even though no one seemed to notice her in the background, her cheeks were infused with cherry red.

Tessa desperately wanted to help her, to

close the gap between Whitley and the other girls, but she knew that would be difficult. It didn't help that Whitley was clearly an introvert and that she came from a different background from the other kids in the group. She even dressed differently than the others, wearing a worn denim skirt and a ruffled shirt that would probably look more natural on someone closer to her grandmother's age. Clothes Tessa imagined the girl had gotten from the bargain bin or secondhand store. They were nothing compared with the sporty designer clothes many of the other teenagers wore.

Giving Whitley any extra attention might backfire on Tessa and bring Whitley nothing but added misery, yet Tessa had a feeling the girl had often been passed over by others only because she didn't put herself forward. She was a sweet girl, and today she was going to have the opportunity to shine, if Tessa had anything to say about it.

First, though, she needed to start with the basics. She'd given a lot of thought to the way she paired off the teenagers, but she knew there was no combination that would be universally approved.

"Whitley," she said, pointing just to the left of center stage. "Why don't you stand in front of this microphone. Matt, you're going to be her partner."

Matt wagged his hands at Tessa aggressively. "No way, man. I don't do—" he paused and leered at Whitley suggestively "—country."

"You'll do what Ms. Applewhite tells you to do," came Cole's deep baritone from behind her. "And you'll do it quickly and without another word. You got that?"

Surprise skittered up her spine, and her skin turned to gooseflesh. How long had Cole been standing there? And why was he here at all after the way he'd left things?

The last time she'd seen him, he'd given her the definite impression he didn't want anything to do with her—or with the project.

And yet here he was, striding across the community center floor, Grayson in his car seat in one hand and a diaper bag over his shoulder. That might have lessened the impact of another man's words, but somehow the fact that Cole carried his son with him didn't detract from his rugged masculinity, or his authority with the teenagers and his innate ability to put them in awe of him.

His gaze narrowed on Matt, and the teenager's jaw twitched with strain.

"Move it," he said when Matt didn't immediately comply with his demand. "And lose the attitude, mister."

It wasn't exactly the way Tessa would have handled it, but right now she had to admit she appreciated the good cop/bad cop support he was giving her, even if she didn't know why he'd suddenly decided to help.

Matt reluctantly took his place beside Whitley. Cole turned to Tessa. The leaden smile on his lips didn't reach his eyes.

That answered one question, apparently. He wasn't over whatever had set him off the other day and made him leave in such a tizzy. But he *was* here now, and this *was* work, so with a great deal of internal effort, she put her own personal feelings aside.

"Did you decide on a musical selection?" Cole asked in an offhanded way.

Seriously? He managed to raise her dander with a single well-placed question. She jerked her chin affirmatively and sent him a look that said everything she wasn't able to say out loud.

Yes, she had chosen music—*no thanks to him.*

He evidently read the message loud and clear, because a flash of guilt zipped through his gaze before he shrugged what to Tessa was a pathetic attempt at an apology. But she supposed it would have to do. For now.

"Why don't I pass out the sheet music to everyone?" he suggested. "I know we didn't talk about this at our meeting, but are you going to accompany them on the piano?"

Accompany would be a bit of a stretch on her best day. She could pick out the notes of a tune on a piano and that was about it. She'd always wanted to play. She'd even started taking lessons her senior year of high school, but she hadn't had the time or money to keep going once she was in college.

Not that he would know that. He was long gone out of her life by then. So, no, she wasn't going to accompany the kids on the piano.

"I brought backup tracks," she said, pointing to the portable CD player she'd toted along with her. "It's a familiar song. I think all the kids know it, or at least the refrain."

Cole nodded. "Harmony?"

"I've worked out a little bit near the end. Mostly it's just back and forth between the guys and girls. Let's listen." She turned on the stereo.

"Y'all know the refrain to this song, right?" Since she'd already talked to the girls about the piece, her question was mostly directed toward the guys. She was relieved when they all nodded. Maybe this would be easier than she'd originally imagined, with or without Cole's help.

"First verse, girls. Second verse, guys. I thought we might use a solo for the bridge."

Cole's eyebrows rose and one side of his lips kicked up in a crooked grin. His glittering gaze made her stomach flutter. "In English, please, for those of us who aren't musically inclined. When did we start talking about *Star Trek?*"

His remark had everyone laughing, including Tessa, though she would rather have been immune to the chemistry between them. Even Whitley cracked a timid smile.

"That would be Sulu, not solo, you moron," she teased. "And the only Enterprise we'll be experiencing is the one where we learn the music and choreography."

She took advantage of the light moment to put her plan into action. She inhaled a deep, calming breath, hoping she was making the right decision. Her next words could either break Whitley out of her shell or seal her off forever.

Tessa knew that with certainty, for she had

once been a girl like Whitley. Leaning toward the shy side. Acting withdrawn, because with a mother in the military, she'd never stayed very long in one place, never made any close friends.

Until she'd found music. Or rather, until music had found her. The spotlight hadn't seemed quite so glaring when she was singing and lost in whatever character she was portraying.

Tessa had heard Whitley singing to herself when she thought no one was around. The girl had some serious skills. Tessa only hoped her peers thought so. It might be the break Whitley needed, just as it had been for Tessa.

"I'll explain more as we go along about what a bridge is within a song, but, Whitley, can I count on you for the solo?"

The teenager's huge brown eyes grew even wider, and she took a giant step backward, shaking her head and waving her hands in dismay.

Tessa smiled, hoping to encourage her to take a chance, to put herself out there just this once. "Let's just see how it goes, shall we? Whitley, you don't have to decide right this second. For the time being, let's focus on the refrain, which we will all be singing together."

She changed the track to the accompaniment without words and sang the first verse for the teenagers while they all listened. Singing was Tessa's sweet spot, and she didn't feel uncomfortable or embarrassed—at least until she glanced Cole's direction, intending to signal for him to make sure the teenagers knew when they should join in.

Her gaze met and locked with Cole's. His blue eyes warmed, and his Adam's apple bobbed as he swallowed hard. For what felt like a lifetime but was probably only a matter of seconds, everything around them faded away. Though the music was still playing and she was still singing, she could no longer hear the background noise—her heart was roaring with music all its own.

She stumbled over the last words of the verse and the moment shattered. Cole effortlessly picked up the melody where she'd left off, his smooth baritone filling the community center with warmth.

She'd missed hearing his singing voice. Despite denying his musical ability, the man had it in spades. He was a natural.

It was how they'd first met. She wondered if he remembered.

"Everyone join in, please," she encouraged

the teens when she remembered she and Cole had a captive audience. The girls started singing, quietly at first and then bolder as the refrain went on. Tessa could even pick out Whitley's lovely soprano in the mix. One of the guys also started singing but quickly cut himself off when he realized that none of the other boys had bothered.

Cole waved at her to stop the music.

"What's the deal, fellows? The girls all understood what they were supposed to be doing, but not one of you guys did? You're making me look bad. We're all singing the refrain together. *All* of us," he reiterated in a voice Tessa was certain had worked remarkably well in his career in the navy. It had a significant effect on the teenagers.

He definitely had the boys' attention, but their second attempt with the chorus yielded little success and no male voices other than Cole's. The guys looked as if they wanted to squirm right out of their skins.

"Out of your comfort zones, are you?" Cole said, evidently having picked up on the same vibe.

"I don't see why we have to do this," Matt complained. The other guys nodded in agreement. "I can't sing."

"No? Have you ever tried? Show of hands, here. Who sings in the shower? In the car? Be honest now."

One by one the teenagers raised their hands until only Matt held back, his fists jammed into the front pockets of his baggy jeans. Tessa had to give him points for maintaining his stubbornness.

"I'm a football player," Matt explained when everyone's eyes turned on him.

"So was I," Cole replied. "But that isn't a very good excuse. It's not like football and singing are mutually exclusive."

"It is where I come from."

"I see." Cole released a breath and gestured for the teens to be seated. "Sit down for a minute. I have a story to tell you."

Grayson made a gurgling sound, and Tessa pulled him out of the car seat, rocking him gently as she waited to hear what Cole would share. She was at least as curious as the teenagers, maybe more so.

"Once upon a time," he started, causing the girls to burst into a fit of giggles. He held up a hand and raised his eyebrows, a smile lining his face. "Once upon a time, I wasn't the old codger you see in front of you now. When I was a senior in high school, I helped lead my football team to win the state finals."

Matt's gaze flashed with a sudden interest. Cole had the rest of the teenagers mesmerized, as well.

"I had friends. Lots of them. Guess you could say I ran with the *in* crowd. But there was one thing I didn't have—something I really wanted."

Grayson started babbling, and Tessa checked the diaper bag for a bottle. She should probably take the baby out of the room so he didn't interrupt Cole's story with his fussing, but she hesitated.

What had he wanted so desperately back then? What has she missed—not known about him?

When he paused, the only sound was Grayson rooting for the bottle. Cole grinned crookedly and winked at her.

"Guess you could say it was more of a some*one* than a something. Let's just say I wanted to get the girl."

Tessa gasped. He was talking about her. *Them.*

"Not just any girl, mind you, but the most beautiful redhead I'd ever laid eyes on. The sweetest, too."

Now he was piling it on a little too thick. She wanted to roll her eyes. She was certain the teenagers would never buy his saccharine story—and yet Cole appeared to have their rapt attention.

"See, the problem was, she wasn't really into sports. Or football players. I couldn't impress her with my skills on the field. She was the star of the theater program. That was quite a barrier, right? I could have let that stop me."

He waited for the teens to nod.

"That's right. I knew it wouldn't be easy, but I've never been the kind of man to take no for an answer."

Tessa's heart had been welling into her throat at Cole's recitation of the all-too-familiar story, but at his last words, it plunged into her stomach like a lead balloon.

He had experienced one *no* in his life—a very public one. And he hadn't even tried to change her mind.

"I figured the easiest way to get this girl to notice me—really notice me—would be to try out for the school musical. You have to understand, I'd never sung a lick of music in my life, at least not out in public where someone could hear me. And you can bet my friends teased me about it. But you know what? I did it, anyway. I stuck my neck out there and got a part."

Tessa's ears were glued to Cole's voice, but she kept her eyes trained on Grayson. She wasn't sure she could look Cole in the face right now. Her old standby—running away from what made her uncomfortable—was pressing at her from all sides. Her skin was itching with the desire to cut out of the room before the teenagers put the whole story together.

Because eventually, they would discover whom Cole was talking about. And that was going to complicate matters. Immensely. Which was why she wanted to pick up and leave right now.

She'd thought she'd learned her lesson, that she had matured beyond the temptation to *run away if it hurt*.

Evidently she wasn't as mature as she'd imagined herself to be.

"You got the lead?" Kaylie asked the question Tessa imagined all the teenagers were wondering.

Cole belted out a laugh. "Nope. I was the understudy, which was perfectly fine for me. I wouldn't have to sing in front of an audience, but I hoped I could still spend time with the girl I liked—rehearse with her from time to time. It didn't work out well, though. Not as I'd imagined. But then something amazing happened. Opening night came, and the lead man caught the flu. At the very last minute, I had to go on in his place."

"For reals?" Matt asked.

"Definitely. It doesn't get any more *real* than having your very first kiss with the love of your life on a stage in front of a couple of hundred people."

Tessa's head jerked up, and she accidentally yanked the bottle from Grayson's hungry lips.

The love of his life?

Grayson wailed in protest, and every eye turned on her. Heat rose from her toes to her eyebrows. She cringed. Blushes didn't look good on redheads.

"Red? You okay?"

There was a gasp from somewhere among the teenagers. She didn't know who was the first to figure it out. But she knew by the rush of voices that followed that they'd caught onto the bombshell factor of the story.

She was that girl.

Tessa tried desperately to refocus her attention on Grayson, but she felt as if her entire world had just tipped on end.

The love of his life, he'd said. Is that what she had been to him? For her part, she'd once thought Cole was that man. If she was honest, she would have to admit she might still be harboring a few lingering feelings, but she was surprised he would still refer to her that way.

Did a person ever completely get over their first love?

Yes. She had. She thought she had. She'd gone years without thinking about Cole. Much. Okay—sometimes. But why should that matter? He was a big part of her past, after all.

And then, when he'd come back into her life and brought his sweet infant son, she suddenly didn't know her own heart anymore. The story of how they'd met was bittersweet at best. Too much had been lost between them. She didn't want to think about it.

"Can I help?" Tessa looked up to find Whitley by her side.

"I— Sure," Tessa stammered, passing her the baby and the bottle. She would rather have had something to do with her hands to keep her busy, but this was the first time Whitley had put herself out there for anything, and Tessa couldn't miss this opportunity, no matter how she was feeling personally.

The teenager's face lit up as she settled Grayson into the curve of her arm and offered him the bottle. The infant rooted and fussed for a moment, and then Whitley started to sing the song they were supposed to have been practicing. To Tessa's surprise, Grayson immediately stopped crying, staring up at Whitley with a keen interest.

In fact, everyone's conversation halted as Whitley's peers stared at her in astonishment. Tessa had known Whitley had a lovely voice, but until that moment, she hadn't realized just how powerful and moving it was.

Whitley appeared oblivious to the attention she was getting. Her entire focus was on the baby in her arms.

"I call *her* as my partner." Matt was the first one to speak up. "Ha. The rest of you guys are out of luck."

All the kids laughed at Matt's sudden change of heart—everyone, that is, except Kaylie. She burst into tears, ran off the stage and bolted out the nearest exit. Tessa cringed. It was all too reminiscent of her own past behavior, except...

"What just happened?" Tessa asked, her gaze finding Cole's.

Cole's expression was grim. "I've got this,"

he said and strode out the door without another word.

Tessa was beyond being able to roll with the punches this afternoon had been throwing at her. She no longer even wanted to try.

"All right, then," she muttered, gesturing for the teenagers to rise to their feet. "Let's take it from the top."

Cole couldn't believe the day of the June BBQ was already upon him. Where had the week gone? He stared at his freshly shaven reflection in the mirror and adjusted the dark brown bolo tie that fastened the collar of his crisp Western shirt. As a wrangler, he didn't usually wear white. It was too easy to get light colors smudged or dirty. He'd had to purchase a new dress shirt from Emerson's just for this occasion.

Tessa had decided that the two of them should match the teenagers, so they all wore black jeans and white shirts. It was a classy gesture, and Cole would never have thought of something like that. He didn't remember Tessa being so organized and detail-oriented back in high school, but he didn't know whether that was simply a trait he'd overlooked in her, or whether her education and her career as a counselor at Redemption Ranch had changed her habits. He'd been so caught up in his youthful feelings for her back then that he suspected he'd missed a lot of things.

The day of the June BBQ had arrived faster than Cole anticipated—not that he ever would have been really ready for it. Grayson was going through a growth spurt that left him perpetually hungry and fussy to boot. Cole was getting about four hours of sleep a night if he was lucky, and his physical exhaustion was starting to get to him. He had been busy working with the teenagers in the stables and on the trails and then tacking on the extra responsibility of practicing the music for their performance.

The late nights were the worst. All he could do was pace up and down the dark hallway with Grayson with nothing to do but run things through his head. Problems always felt worse in the dead of night, and thinking about the barbecue was no exception. He had no idea how he was going to get through the event with his heart intact. It took every ounce of his willpower to push his anxiety continuously to the back of his mind, but he refused to dwell on it. He'd deal with whatever issues arose when the time came.

Grayson wasn't the only one keeping Cole up at night. He was worried about Kaylie, as well. She wasn't on an emotionally even keel, and yet she continued to insist he keep her secret for her. Private, just between the two of them and Dr. Delia.

When he'd caught up with Kaylie after she'd bolted, he'd done everything but get down on his knees and beg her to come clean to Tessa, but to no avail.

Cole still berated himself for bringing Grayson with him the day of the first practice. If he'd thought it all the way through, he would have realized how difficult seeing the baby would be for Kaylie, but he hadn't recognized it at the time. And anyway, he didn't have a babysitter other than his father. What was a man to do?

At least he'd convinced Kaylie to see Dr. Delia, reminding her of the doctor-patient confidentiality that would keep her secret safe. He'd even taken her to the doctor's office himself on one of her free afternoons. He hated feeling as if they were sneaking around behind Tessa's back and Alexis's, as well. He didn't like the idea of keeping the truth from either of them. But he was doing what he could for Kaylie, and for now, that would have to be enough. She was starting to trust him. Maybe eventually she'd have enough confidence in him to allow Tessa into the loop.

Kaylie and her baby had checked out okay at the doctor's, thankfully, other than being slightly underweight for her late stage of pregnancy. Cole had pulled Dr. Delia aside and voiced his concern that Kaylie was hardly showing, but other than mentioning a few restrictions for late-stage pregnancy, Delia assured him all was well.

That was something good, at least. Wasn't it?

He shook his head at his reflection. It wasn't nearly enough, but it would have to do for now.

He pushed a comb through his hair, trying to tame the wavy wayward locks with gel, but didn't have much success. He supposed it didn't matter in the long run. His cowboy hat would negate his work in five minutes. Now that his once-neat military haircut had grown out, he looked as if he belonged riding out on the range, even clean shaven and well dressed.

He only wanted to look nice for Tessa's sake. He wasn't the kind of man who gave much thought to outward appearances, especially his own. He supposed he also wanted to look good for the teenagers—show them that they had his full support. Tessa and the kids deserved to know he had their backs in this performance and, well, everything they did together.

It wasn't Tessa's fault he was wrestling through his own issues. In the process, he had given her a whale of a hard time lately. Despite their past, she didn't deserve that kind of attitude from him. She had her hands full with those hormonal teenage girls and prank-pulling teenage boys without him adding to the pressure. He vowed to treat her better, and today at the barbecue was a good place to start.

"Ready, little man?" Settling his cowboy hat on his head, he slid Grayson into the carrier strapped to his chest and slung the diaper bag over his shoulder. It occurred to him that the diaper bag didn't embarrass him anymore—not even a tiny gnaw at his male ego or pride. He chuckled.

When he arrived at the community green a few minutes later, the park was already buzzing with activity. Folks were arriving, their arms laden with food. Local paramedics and best friends Ben and Zach had dug a pit the day before and were roasting a whole pig.

Cup O' Jo's was providing a delicious array of Phoebe Hawkins's baked goods, and the other townsfolk brought potluck, all of their families' favorite dishes to share. One would imagine they could end up with a hundred bags of potato chips and nothing to dip them in, but oddly enough, the potluck fare always tended to work out fairly well, even without any formal organization.

The festivities—picnic games for both adults and children, music, dancing, and the best part of all to Cole, the eating—wouldn't begin for another hour yet, but many folks, Cole included, arrived early to help set up.

Folding tables from the nearby community church were being toted out and unloaded, with Pastor Shawn and his wife, Heather, facilitating the entire process. Jo Spencer arrived bearing a large stack of colorful red-checked tablecloths from the café. Cole helped her spread them across the broad tables, securing them with special clips to brace them against the inevitable Texas breeze. Soon there'd be so many dishes on the tables, there would be no need for the clips. Cole's mouth was watering already. If there was one thing he could say for certain about Serendipity, it was that they excelled at their good, down-home country cooking.

The town council had brought in a popular band for the gig. It was a town tradition. Most events in Serendipity were covered by local musicians, but at the June BBQ, the town splurged on outside music so that all the locals could dance.

Cole swallowed hard. He'd started that particular tradition twelve years ago when he'd brought in Tessa's favorite singing group as a special surprise for her—right before he'd proposed to her in front of the whole town. She'd not only rejected him, but also bolted off the green as if her tail was on fire.

To this day, he didn't know what had gone wrong. He'd honestly thought she'd been expecting him to put a ring on her finger, and he'd most certainly anticipated her acceptance of his proposal.

That hadn't happened.

"Cole, sweetie, your face is as red as the checks on this tablecloth. This isn't easy for you, is it, dear?" Jo's voice and her expression were the epitome of compassion and empathy. She was like a second mother to most of the town, Cole included. He'd grown up under her guidance and supervision. Cup O'

Jo's was the place to be when folks needed help or advice. She might be the lead grinder of the gossip mill, but she was also the strongest link in Serendipity's prayer chain—and the most kind and intuitive woman Cole had ever known.

"Yes. It's rough," he admitted, cringing inwardly. He saw no point in denying the truth. If Jo remembered how the events transpired between him and Tessa twelve years ago at the June BBQ, more than likely others did, as well.

This would no doubt be an excruciating day for him and Tessa both. Suddenly Cole could see the wisdom of the way Alexis and Jo had bound them together over the music project with the youth. Folks would see them working together and, ideally, realize the past was just that—the past.

They had both moved on. They were over it.

"May the Almighty bless you but good, young man. Y'all are doing all right."

"We?"

"You and Tessa. And Grayson. You're a good man, Cole Bishop. And a wonderful father."

Cole couldn't meet Jo's eyes. "You give me too much credit," he muttered, yanking his end of the tablecloth and accidentally jerking it out of Jo's hands.

"Oh, dear," she breathed.

"Sorry."

"Talk to her."

"What? Who?" he asked, although he already knew the answer.

"Tessa. Tell her how you feel."

He shook his head. "I don't—"

"Hmmph," Jo snorted, planting her fists on her ample hips. "Are you really going to stand there and finish that sentence, us being in God's presence and all? He's everywhere, you know, not just in church. He's in your heart. Don't say what you don't mean."

"Well, even if I do feel something—and I'm not admitting to anything, so don't go throwing coal in the engine of the gossip train just yet—I don't see how talking about it is going to help. There's too much between Tessa and me that was left unsaid for too long."

"Sometimes you have to go back before you can go forward, dear. The talkin' that should have happened years ago but didn't, for starters. That needs to happen. I know it scares the socks off you, but Tessa might surprise you. High time you two made peace with each other. The real thing, not just a rigid truce."

Cole lifted his hat and threaded his fingers through his hair. He wasn't going to be admitting to fear anytime soon, but Jo was right about the rest of it, and she was probably the only one in Serendipity wise enough and brave enough to speak the truth to him.

"Agreed. It won't be easy, but I'll talk to her."

"Today?"

Cole wasn't sure he was ready for any kind of confrontation with Tessa. He hadn't had time to think through what he was going to say, and he wasn't the kind of man to go off half-cocked.

Oh, who was he kidding? He'd had twelve years to think on it. Jo was right. Now was the time for action.

"I'll speak to her as soon as—"

"Great. She's right over there, talking to her father." Jo pointed across the green. "From the looks of things, Tessa might appreciate being rescued right about now."

Once again, Jo was right on. Tessa was absorbed in a heated conversation. Both she and her dad appeared strained. Her father was frowning as he spoke, and Tessa had her arms wrapped tightly around her middle—a tell Cole well recognized even after all these years.

"I'll take Grayson," Jo said, lifting her arms toward the baby. "The teens won't be performing for another hour at least, and there's plenty of other folks who can help with the settin' up. You go do what needs to be done."

His heart in this throat and his pulse roaring in his ears, he squared his shoulders and headed toward Tessa. His emotions were tentative, maybe even a little bit apprehensive, but his steps were not.

If he was going to commit to this thing, he needed to be all in, mind, body and spirit. Completely focused.

And totally vulnerable.

It wasn't a comfortable place for him to be.

"Bart," he said, extending his hand to Tessa's father. "Good to see you."

Cole's words were more of a polite concession than a precise truth. He didn't like the way Bart was scowling at his daughter, and it was all he could do not to tell the man so. If Bart had a problem with Tessa, there was no need to air it in a public venue.

"Did you hear what we've got going today?" Cole laid a supportive hand on Tessa's shoulder, showing her—and Bart—where he stood in this obvious game of wills. He half expected Tessa to tense under his touch, maybe even pull away, but instead she leaned into him, absorbing his strength.

"That's what we were just talking about," Tessa replied, looking as if she'd eaten something that disagreed with her. "I was just telling him how hard our teens have worked to put on their performance today."

"And I was telling her that she's wasting her time on these kids. No musical number is going to turn juvenile delinquents into law-abiding citizens."

"There's a lot more to it than that," Cole said. "Tessa—"

Tessa cut him off with a sharp jerk of her chin.

"Tessa," Cole insisted, "makes a difference in these teenagers' lives. Many of them have never experienced real love—God's love and human love. Tessa points them to God and showers them with His love. And hers. I can't think of many other careers you can say that about."

He stared Bart down, daring him to disagree. Bart glanced at Tessa and opened his mouth as if to argue, but when his gaze returned to Cole, he clamped his jaw shut.

Tessa quivered and Cole stepped closer to her, enveloping her with his arm. She fit perfectly under his shoulder. He didn't remember that from his youth. He supposed maybe he'd grown some since then, physically as well as emotionally, and for Tessa's sake, he was glad that was true.

She was a strong woman, but she was also extremely sensitive. Not to mention the fact that it was her father getting down on her. Fathers and children were a special dynamic, and in this case not a good one. Didn't Bart realize he was hurting her by his careless words and actions?

"It's almost time for us to get the teens together," Cole said. "If you don't mind, Bart, Tessa and I have a few items to go over before the performance begins." Though he didn't feel it, he smiled at Bart. "Keep an open mind, sir. I think you'll be impressed by Tessa's hard work with these kids. I know I am."

He didn't wait for Bart to formulate a comeback. Instead, he guided Tessa gently but firmly in the opposite direction.

Tessa waited until they were well away from her father before she whirled on him. "Do you want to tell me what that was all about?"

He cocked a brow and kicked up one side of his lips. "What? No, 'Thank you, Cole'?"

Her gaze widened, and for a moment he lost

himself in the emerald of her eyes. He waited for her to unload on him—how she didn't need rescuing. How she was doing just fine on her own. How he ought to mind his own business. And probably a lot of other things about him that she'd think but never say aloud.

"Thank you, Cole." It was little more than a whisper, and her gaze dropped to the floor. "I don't know why my dad gets that way sometimes. You'd think after all these years he'd get over the fact that I changed majors and am doing a job I really love. But occasionally he just gets—"

"Stubborn," Cole finished for her. "Prideful—and unreasonable. Traits males all seem to have in common. Getting our backs bent all out of whack when we should be listening and trying to understand stuff."

"Stuff?" she repeated, her gaze rising and her eyes clouding with confusion. "Are we still talking about my father here?"

Cole shook his head. "No. No, we're not. See, you figured that out because you were listening."

She chuckled. "They don't call it women's intuition for nothing."

"Great. Then it's settled. We don't need to have this conversation, after all."

"This conversation? Why do I feel like you have an agenda here?"

"I do. We do. Walk with me?" He gestured to the outskirts of the community green, which was surrounded by a gravel pathway marked with several iron benches.

"Where's Grayson?"

"In Jo's capable hands. We won't be interrupted, if that's what you're worried about."

"Grayson would never be an interruption."

Cole laughed. "I meant Jo." He placed his hand on the small of Tessa's back to guide her away from the ever-growing crowd.

"This day isn't going to be easy for either of us, is it?" she murmured, but it was a thoughtful comment and not an accusatory one.

"The first Saturday in June has always been a problem for me. I expect it may be the same for you, especially since you've been living in Serendipity for a while."

She nodded. "I usually make an excuse to avoid the whole thing. This year I don't have that choice—and I suspect that's exactly the way Alexis and Jo wanted it."

"You always have a choice, Tessa. You do now, and you did back then. I'll admit I was an overconfident kid at the time and I didn't even realize it. It didn't even occur to me that you might reject my marriage proposal or I certainly wouldn't have made it into a public display."

"I know you went to a lot of trouble for me. I appreciate that now, looking back on it. You brought in my favorite singing group. Planned out every detail of what you thought was going to be the perfect proposal."

Cole chuckled drily. "Well, it obviously wasn't the *perfect* proposal, seeing as you turned me down and bolted from the scene."

"I regret my actions that day."

"Rejecting me or bolting from the scene?"

"Both. I had to turn you down, Cole. I *had* to. But I wish we had been able to talk about it before you left for the navy."

"Yeah, I guess I did my fair share of bolting as well, didn't I?"

"I honestly believed you'd come after me that day. That we'd be able to work through our problems."

"Is that what you were waiting for?" Cole's spine stiffened. "Were you playing some kind of game with me?"

"What? No. No! I would never do that."

He let out the breath he'd been holding. "Then explain it to me. I wasn't ready to hear your reasoning back then, but I am now. Why did you reject me? We'd been talking about getting married and having a future together."

"That's just it. We spoke of the future, but you never mentioned enlisting in the navy. Not until after the fact."

"I didn't?"

"Well, maybe in general terms—wanting to see the world, thinking there must be more excitement outside of our little community. Call me naïve, but I thought those were just the aimless ramblings of a restless teenage boy. I believed if we were going to get married and have a family, it would be here in Serendipity."

Cole scoffed. "In a way, my words were aimless ramblings, or at least youthful ones. Adulthood isn't quite what you expect it to be when you're looking at it from the teenage end of things, is it? Where there were no restrictions or limitations to your thinking and nothing to hold you back from your dreams?"

They reached a park bench. Cole gestured for her to sit and then slid beside her with his arm resting across the top of the bench.

"I still don't understand why you didn't talk to me before you enlisted," she said. "If you really believed we were going to marry each other, I would have thought we'd discuss something that important as a couple. If I had accepted your proposal, your joining the navy would have affected me as much as it did you. Maybe more, in some ways."

"You'd think I would have considered that, wouldn't you?" He pursed his lips, only now truly seeing his actions through her eyes. All these years he'd placed the blame squarely on her shoulders for leading him on and then tossing him away. Now he realized it wasn't quite that simple.

"I couldn't do it." Tessa shifted her gaze to somewhere over his left shoulder.

"Do what? Marry me?"

"Marry a military man. Not after watching my parents' marriage disintegrate over the stress of my mother's multiple deployments. Not after having to move from base to base and school to school without ever really being able to put down roots. Not after grieving for a mother who was killed in the line of duty."

Cole's gut clenched as if he'd been punched. He hadn't seen it—any of it. He'd been an immature and self-absorbed kid with his head in the clouds and his feet not even remotely close to being solidly planted on earth. And he'd thought he would be a good husband and father?

"I couldn't have proposed to you in any worse way, could I? Starting off by announcing my enlistment to you and the whole town and then pulling out a ring and expecting you to act surprised and pleased by it."

"Oh, I was surprised, all right. Just not in the way you imagined."

"I should say not."

Their conversation lapsed into an uneasy silence as they each explored their own memories and emotions. The expression on Tessa's face, so raw and painful, tore at Cole's heart. He reached out and gently smoothed away the worry lines on her face with the pad of his thumb.

"We thought we were ready. We weren't," Tessa said, sniffling. Her eyes were glassy, but no tears fell.

"No," Cole agreed. "We weren't. We were just a couple of immature teenagers, not much different than the kids we're mentoring now."

Tessa's gaze widened, but then she nodded. "No, I suppose we weren't."

"I did love you, you know." He almost slipped and said *do*—in the present tense, and not the past.

Where had that come from?

"Yeah," she replied, sighing deeply. "Me, too."

"If we'd married, you probably wouldn't have gone to college and discovered your gift for counseling teenagers."

"And had we been more circumspect, you might not have joined the navy, might never have seen the world. Might never have had Grayson."

Cole cringed. If only she knew Grayson was conceived in the first place precisely because he'd been mourning the loss of their relationship. Only an idiot, a weak man, lost control the way he had, drinking himself into oblivion.

But the alternative, marrying Tessa right out of high school, seemed equally unreasonable to him. He would have been holding her back from becoming the woman she was now, helping any number of teenagers to move on to better their lives.

"Even if we'd made different choices at the time, it never could have worked at all, could it?" he asked.

A single tear trailed down Tessa's cheek, but she swiftly and silently brushed it away. She looked down and shook her head. "No, I don't suppose so. You're right. We never would have worked out."

Chapter Eight

Tessa couldn't get away from Cole fast enough, but unfortunately, she was obligated to spend at least part of the afternoon with him. The sooner she could get the teenagers on stage, the sooner she could make her excuses and get far, far away from the disaster that was the June BBQ. It occurred to her that maybe she was running away again, but how could she stand to be here after all Cole had revealed about his heart?

Even if we'd made different choices at the time, it never could have worked at all.

His words were true enough, but that didn't make them any less painful, like a sharp knife to her already aching heart.

With Cole back in town and their collaboration on the teens' musical number, she'd known the barbecue was going to be emotional for her, even before they'd had their heart-to-heart conversation. She'd had no idea how topsy-turvy it would be. Her stomach was churning as if she'd just exited a roller coaster—one that had gone upside down and backward.

She'd known there was no hope of a relationship between her and Cole. This wasn't news to her. And until today, she would have denied the thought had even crossed her mind that she might want to try again.

But in one shocking moment as she'd sat across from Cole with their gazes locked and their hearts open, she'd realized that was not completely true. She *did* still harbor feelings for him. Maybe they had never left her. Granted, it was a different kind of feeling, one that encompassed where they had been, where they were now and where they were going.

Too bad she'd experienced that emotional epiphany at the very moment Cole was denying such a love could ever or would ever work out between them. Talk about the irony to end all ironies.

Cole might be right about some of the things he'd said. Their relationship could very well have been an unmitigated disaster if they'd said their I do's as a young couple. In a town as small and close-knit as Serendipity, many folks married young and had long and prosperous relationships and happy families despite, or maybe even because of, the challenges they faced.

Would she and Cole have been different if they'd married? Would their lives have taken other roads? Tessa couldn't honestly imagine her life without the therapy work she did at Redemption Ranch.

And yet—a life with Cole would have been something special. Loving him. Bearing his children. Growing old with him. She couldn't help but wonder what that life might have been like. She already knew he was a wonderful father and had no doubt he would be a good and faithful husband to the woman blessed to become his wife.

Even now, only minutes after their heartbreaking conversation had ended, Cole already had Grayson in his arms and was proudly showing him off to the community. He beamed whenever he looked at his son. His luminous blue eyes would simply alight with joy. Those long nights pacing the hallway with a colicky baby had only drawn him closer to the infant.

She shook her head and scoffed at herself. As Cole had just said, she wasn't a starry-eyed teenager anymore, and yet here she was, mooning over the rugged cowboy like a lovesick calf.

She pulled her emotions back, burying them deep inside her. Speaking of teenagers— she had a job to do. She was grateful to have something productive to take her mind off her conversation with Cole. She could mourn the loss of that love later, in private.

Right now she had teenagers to rustle together and a musical performance to direct. As she found the teens and guided them toward the stage on the green, Cole handed Grayson off to his father so he could set up the mics and test them for sound quality.

It wasn't long before she could hear the teens' nervous chatter over the milling of the crowd. She waved to get their attention and made a slicing motion across her throat with her index finger, mouthing the words *live microphones*.

The teens were banded in a tight group on stage. Without any prompting on Tessa's part, Cole split them up into the couples they'd been practicing with over the past week and then gave Tessa a thumbs-up to begin the performance. After a few last-minute, hastily whispered directions, the teens were ready to do their thing. Cole scrambled off the stage and moved to stand beside her.

He brushed her elbow with his arm, and she felt as if he'd shocked her. She was excruciatingly aware of his every movement. His presence was tangible even when he was standing perfectly still beside her.

"Ready?" he asked, his finger hovering over the play button on a sound system that was nothing more than a hastily hacked rig of their portable CD player and someone's home theater surround-sound system.

Taking a deep breath to calm her shaky nerves, she raised her hand like a conductor and waited until she was certain she had all of the teenagers' attention. The crowd on the green had stopped talking and was eagerly awaiting the performance. Even Matt, who was usually the one goofing around when he was supposed to be serious, stopped fidgeting and stood perfectly still, his hands resting lightly on Whitley's waist, ready to perform the minimal choreography they'd managed to work out over the week's worth of rehearsals.

"And…go," Cole whispered, punching the button.

The intro to the music began, and the girls

successfully launched into the first verse, growing stronger and more confident with each line. The boys had just joined in for the chorus when she felt Cole's hands gently kneading her shoulders.

"Your shoulders are as stiff as mine feel," he murmured with a low chuckle. "I've got to admit I was worried about how this thing was going to go off. I'm a bundle of nerves. You'd think I was the one up there performing. But the kids are doing great."

Tessa nodded, feeling as if all the oxygen had faded from the atmosphere—and not because she'd been worried about how the kids were going to do in their performance. There was that, of course, but it was Cole's warm breath fanning her cheek that had her struggling to catch a breath.

"These kids can really sing," Cole said. "Not like me. Remember? My first time singing on the stage was a last-minute Hail Mary. My voice was so shaky that night. I'm surprised anyone could understand a word I sang."

She remembered, all right, but he was wrong about his voice. It had been perfect. Mesmerizing, at least for her.

"Here we go for round two," he said. "Let's get 'em, guys."

The boys jumped into the second verse with a cheerful abandon that surprised even Tessa. She'd figured they'd probably perform better with the entire town watching them, and she'd been right. They acted as if they were really into it—and into the girls who were their partners.

Even Matt. Maybe especially Matt, as he whirled Whitley out and then back again before she stepped up to the microphone to sing her solo.

Her pure soprano had more than one audience member oohing and ahhing, and Tessa smiled.

Personal issues aside, this day was a win.

"Yes!" Cole exclaimed, pumping his fist in the air as the teenagers finished the song in a harmony that was…actual harmony. In tune and everything.

The teens joined hands and stepped forward to take a bow. All of them were smiling at the response of the roaring crowd. Nothing like a good audience to make a performer feel like a million bucks, and all of her kids were worth at least that much. Matt gently insisted that Whitley step forward to take a bow on her own and enjoy a round of applause for her solo. Then the teens joined hands once again to take a final bow. Cole whistled and cheered louder than anyone else on the green.

Tessa had to admit she was surprised at Cole's unabashed reaction to the performance. He'd been present at all the rehearsals but hadn't shown much interest in the production. He certainly hadn't acted remotely like the man who was currently high-fiving every one of the teens and telling them how well they'd nailed their song.

The kids were eating it up. Clearly Cole's affirmation meant a lot to them. They looked up to him. Tessa wondered if Cole knew just how successful a mentor he had become.

Soon the teenagers disbursed, and Cole was back at Tessa's side. When she turned toward him, he whooped and wrapped his arms around her waist, picking her clean off the ground and twirling her around and around until she was dizzy. Or maybe the light-headedness came simply from being in his arms.

"That was awe-some," he said, breaking the word into two distinct syllables.

Tessa laughed despite herself. "Yes, it kind of was, wasn't it?"

"I never would have thought."

Tessa suddenly became aware of the way

her arms wrapped around his neck and the strength of his shoulders. "Thought what?"

"How great it would feel to see our kids succeed at something like that."

Her heart welled, not only from seeing his pride, but because he had referred to them as *our* kids. Finally, he was getting it, starting to understand just how incredible it was to be a mentor.

"Cole?"

"Hmm?" He bent his head on the pretense of listening to her, and his face was buried in her hair. "You smell just like I remember. Like when the lavender bushes bloom in the springtime."

If she could have stopped time at that moment, she would have—there in his arms with him whispering sweetness into her ear. But life went on, and if they weren't careful they would make a spectacle of themselves.

"Put me down. My feet aren't touching the ground."

In more ways than one.

"Oops." He laughed and then set her down so suddenly that she overcorrected and nearly lost her balance. Fortunately, he saw her waver and swiftly reached for her shoulders, keeping a gentle hold on her until she found her feet again.

"Okay, then." She released the breath she'd been unconsciously holding.

"Sorry," he said, one corner of his lips kicking up. "I guess I got a little carried away there for a moment."

So had she.

"I didn't realize it until the teens were up there singing just how much I'd hoped they would succeed. For their sakes, not mine," he clarified.

Tessa smiled softly. "That's because you've become invested in them."

He angled his hat up. "I have, haven't I?"

"They're blessed to have a man like you in their lives." She dropped her eyes, unable to meet his shimmering gaze. "I'm glad you came back to Serendipity."

"Yeah?" He tipped her chin up with his index finger. Their gazes locked. His eyes were swirling with emotions, so many that Tessa couldn't pick one from another. His voice lowered, emerging subdued and husky. "Me, too."

Cole's father, Ford, approached, bouncing Grayson in one arm. "My grandson loved the song, especially that young lady Whitley." He turned his smile to Tessa. "Reminds me of another pretty teenage girl with a remarkable voice."

Tessa blushed at Ford's compliment.

"I'm proud of you, son," Ford continued, slapping Cole on the back with his free hand. Then he enveloped Tessa in a quick hug. "Proud of the pair of you."

Tessa's heart welled with emotion, a combination of honor and pain. If only her own father could see the good in what she was doing.

Marcus approached and complimented them, and then to her surprise, her father stepped into her line of vision. He brushed a hand back through his hair, a nervous gesture.

"I may have been wrong about this," he admitted. How he made his apology sound like a grumble was beyond her, but she was over the moon that he'd seen even a glimpse of the promise of the career that consumed her life. "The kids were good."

"Thanks, Dad." It was a start, and for now, it was enough.

"I think I'd like to hear another musical number," Cole's father boomed. "An encore of sorts."

Cole shook his head. "Sorry, Dad. That's all we've got. I guess we should have guessed the community might want more than one song from the teenagers, but they learned only one."

Ford's eyebrows rose, and his eyes glittered with mischief. "I wasn't talking about the kids, as good as they were. Hey, Jo?" He waved Jo Spencer over to join the conversation. "Since the teenagers were so well received, what do you think about having their directors perform a song for us?"

Jo's bright orange T-shirt had the word *Roasted* swirled over the front. The word was well-placed. Tessa imagined she and Cole would be well-done by the time this day was over. When Jo clapped in delight at the idea and Marcus whooped loud enough to turn the whole crowd's attention to them, Tessa's stomach sank to the floor. They'd reached the point of no return, now that Ford had enlisted Jo in his idea.

Her gaze caught Cole's. He had the same deer-caught-in-the-headlights expression on his face that she imagined she had on hers. Surely Ford didn't mean—

"What was the name of that song I liked so much?" Ford tapped his finger against his chin. "The one you guys did in high school from that different version of *Phantom*." Ford's grin widened, and he winked at her.

"'You Are Music,'" Cole supplied, sounding downright miserable. "From the Kopit and Yeston version."

Tessa cringed. He didn't have to go and offer up the song. And anyway, how could Ford possibly think this was a good idea? Sharing his suggestion with Jo was paramount to adding kindling to an already roaring fire—one that was burning her cheeks.

"It's been twelve years, Dad," Cole objected. "I don't even remember all the lyrics. And besides, we don't have a soundtrack to back us up. There's no way we could sing such a demanding song a cappella."

Never mind a soundtrack. Tessa was quite certain she didn't have a *voice*. She couldn't utter a single squeak in protest, much less sing an entire song.

Jo waved the teenagers closer. "You kids all want to hear Cole and Tessa sing a duet, don't you?"

The clamoring response from the teens was immediate and crazy loud, drawing the attention and interest of any of the people milling around on the green who weren't already hovering to find out what was going on in their circle. Soon it appeared that everyone at the barbecue was aware of the request—and were raucously insisting that Cole and Tessa fulfill it.

Didn't they realize how vocally challenging the song was? And that was if they had time to warm up their voices and find some background accompaniment.

That was to say nothing of the emotional complications that would rise to the surface, were they to sing the duet together.

"Go," Ford insisted, gently bumping her shoulder with his. Grayson, picking up on the excitement, babbled and flapped his arms. "See what I mean?" Ford asked with a laugh. "Your public awaits, my dear."

It wasn't the public Tessa was worried about.

Cole's jaw was tight as he reached for her hand. "You know as well as I do that we're not going to get out of this."

Not unscathed, they weren't.

She followed Cole as he ascended the stairs to the stage. She wanted to pull back, draw away. Cole must have sensed her continued reluctance, because he squeezed her hand and tossed back a reassuring smile.

"We can do this," he affirmed.

"Maybe you can, but I'm not so certain,"

she hissed back under her breath. "It's not like I've been practicing my scales."

"Yeah, me neither. I've never been a singer. But folks here don't expect perfection, Tessa. They just want us to make a good effort."

He was right, of course. Even if they fudged a little on the melody or lyrics, it was highly doubtful anyone would notice. The Kopit and Yeston version of *Phantom* wasn't a particularly well-known musical. No one would notice if they forgot some of the words.

It was all about chemistry between the two characters, and she and Cole had that in spades. No problem there.

He leaned in close to her ear. "Here goes nothing. I'll try not to start too high or we'll both be in trouble."

He squeezed her hand one more time and then turned and walked to the other side of the stage. He paused for a moment and simply breathed. Then he met her gaze. He offered her an encouraging smile.

And then he started to sing.

Funny that he didn't consider himself a musician. His beautiful baritone sent shivers down her spine. But it was more than that. The moment he stepped toward her, reaching out a pleading hand that matched his voice and the lyrics, he *became* Erik, the tortured, disfigured man who longed for beauty in his life.

In high school he'd worn a mask and a cape, but now he needed neither. Even his cowboy hat couldn't distract her from the character he'd become. She'd expected her thoughts to fly back to the night they'd first met on the stage, but when their gazes locked and she joined her voice to his, there was no past between them. Only the present moment, the music and the almost tangible chemistry between them. She felt as if she could reach out and touch it.

His Erik, her Christine, somehow swirled into the very real love story between her and Cole.

The crowd was moved to silence, but it wouldn't have mattered if they'd been roaring at the tops of their lungs. For Tessa there was only Cole.

His voice. His gaze. His love.

The song drew toward its close and Cole drew toward her, reaching for her. He framed her face with his hands, his thumbs lightly brushing across her cheekbones as he gazed down at her.

The air seemed to leave Tessa's lungs. She had no idea how she continued to sing, but her voice was strong, matching Cole's in tone and intensity.

They reached the last note. Held it. Ended it together as one, even though neither one of them signaled the break.

It could have been over then—should have been. But ever so slowly, he tilted his head and leaned toward her, his heart glistening in his blue eyes. He gave her plenty of time and opportunity to stop him, to pull away, but she could no more prevent this moment from happening than stop the earth from spinning on its axis.

She closed her eyes as his mouth hovered over hers. She desperately wanted to close off all of her senses except for one. She wanted to feel the brush of his lips over hers with every part of her being.

Finally, their lips softly met. Once. Twice. And then again, this time lingering, with more strength and intensity.

She'd forgotten how sweet and tender Cole's kiss could be. Without conscious thought, she wrapped her arms around his neck, pulling him closer and returning his emotion, expressing everything she'd been so carefully holding back.

His kiss was like coming home again after

a long absence. Warm and wonderful and totally familiar, and yet paradoxically completely new.

Together, they were greater than the sum of their individual parts. Like the duet they'd just finished singing, their entire lives came together, rich in tone, sweet in harmony.

She was so lost in Cole's kiss that she wasn't immediately aware that the teenagers had ascended to the stage and surrounded them, hooting and cheering for the public display of affection she and Cole were exhibiting.

Mortification filtered through her in an instant. Not only were the teenagers watching them, but practically every resident of Serendipity was clapping for them. She jumped back out of Cole's arms, placing both palms over her burning cheeks.

Cole looked dazed for a moment as he looked around at the teenagers accosting him, but then he threw back his head and laughed.

Laughed.

Oh, what had she done? She would never live this down if she lived to be a hundred years old. The town had a long memory—long enough to attach her history with Cole with what had just happened on the stage today.

And her teenagers?

She might well have lost all the respect she'd worked so hard to gain with them. Throwing herself at Cole with such blatant abandon was hardly the action of a responsible adult in charge of young people.

She hadn't been thinking. Her feelings had overwhelmed her.

She had ruined everything. The song in her heart had ended.

She clamped a hand over her mouth to hold back a sob and turned away from Cole and the teenagers. She didn't run away, but she walked as fast as she could and with as much dignity as she could muster. She had to get somewhere, anywhere, away from the crowd before she completely lost her composure.

Even as she left the scene, she knew she was doing the one thing she'd promised herself she would never do again.

She was running away.

One minute Cole was sharing a laugh with the teenagers over his admittedly overenthusiastic theatrical performance, and the next thing he knew, he was looking for Tessa and she was nowhere to be found.

She'd probably sought a quiet corner to try and pull herself together, and he understood why. To the audience, and much to the delight of the teenagers watching them, he and Tessa had shared a romantic stage kiss, but Cole knew it was much more than that.

They had shared their hearts.

Cole had forgotten what a rush it was to be on stage singing, inhabiting another character, someone who was nothing like him. But in this case, life had certainly brought him a long way around. Now, as an adult, he could empathize with the Phantom's desperate desire to find beauty in his life. Cole had made a mess out of his life. He'd become disfigured in his own way.

But then, despite his failings, he'd found beauty.

In Grayson.

In *Tessa*.

He'd known the moment his lips met hers that this was no stage kiss for the benefit of the audience, or even a wild and crazy tender blast from their past. When she'd wrapped her arms around his neck, she'd silently returned every emotion he was communicating to her.

It was their present. And their future.

It was love.

Not the selfish, immature feelings of an eighteen-year-old boy who had no idea what it meant to give of himself, both his heart and his life, to another person.

This time he was ready to offer Tessa everything in him, to put her needs and desires ahead of his own. There was nothing in the world he wanted more than once again to ask her to be his wife, to welcome her into his heart and his life—and Grayson's, too. He knew he and Grayson were a package deal, which would probably put off most women, but Tessa wasn't most women. He'd seen how much she cared for Grayson. His son wouldn't be a deal breaker. He'd be icing on the cake, making their union even sweeter.

Yet he was getting ahead of himself here. He felt as if he'd made a commitment, a promise, the moment their lips met. But the words still needed to be said, the question still needed to be asked, and properly this time.

He had the engagement ring he'd bought for Tessa all those years ago still tucked in the top drawer of his dresser. He'd thought about selling it but could never find the will to do so, not even when he was at his angriest with her. He'd supposed he was being sentimental, but now he wondered if God had different plans for that ring all along.

One thing was for certain—he wasn't going

to propose to her in a public place. This time he'd choose someplace quiet and romantic, with just the two of them present when he asked her to be his wife.

The teenagers were joshing around with him and giving him a hard time about kissing Tessa, but he was filled with too much joy to care.

Until he spotted Tessa outside the green, heading down the sidewalk and away from the celebration in progress. She should have been here by his side, accepting kudos for a job well done. Instead, she was—

Leaving.

Playing that old familiar trump card. When something upset Tessa, she simply walked away from it. Sometimes even ran. He could tell from the set of her shoulders that she was tense, and the quiver in her step suggested to him that she might even be crying. He knew her well enough by now to interpret her moods, even when he could see her only from the back at a distance.

Why wasn't she as happy as he was? Had she not felt the same connection he had when they'd kissed?

Yes. He knew she'd felt it. She'd both taken and given when they'd kissed. That kind of chemistry—the kind that went far beyond the physical and burrowed into a man's, or a woman's, heart and soul—that was a once-in-a-lifetime feeling.

It was Tessa whom his heart was seeking. It had always been Tessa.

He wasn't going to make the same mistake he'd made as a teenager. He was going to chase after her and have it out with her if need be. He would listen—really *listen*—to her thoughts, feelings, fears and dreams. And then he would prove his love for her in whatever way she needed him to.

She was headed toward Redemption Ranch, although the homestead was located several miles out of Serendipity proper. She'd arrived in the van with the teenagers in tow, which was probably why she was out walking now. She couldn't very well take the kids' only motorized form of transportation back to the ranch.

No worries. He had his truck with him. He wasn't going to let her walk all the way back to the ranch by herself.

"Hey, Cole?"

Cole was fishing his keys out of his pocket when Whitley's tentative voice stopped him.

Matt stood right behind her, and they both appeared worried about something.

Cole hoped they hadn't seen Tessa leave in a huff. Now was not a good time for him to have to explain the past to them. Not when he was in a hurry to catch up with her and make things right.

"It's Kaylie," Matt said.

Adrenaline buzzed through Cole's veins at the mention of Kaylie's name. He took a quick glance at the crowd but didn't see the girl.

"What about her? Is she hurt?"

"I don't know," Whitley said. "I don't think so. But Matt and I saw her take off a little while ago, and she hasn't come back."

"She took off?" Cole echoed. "Where to?"

"We don't know," Matt replied. Whitley was shaking her head, and Matt placed a reassuring hand on her shoulder. "We thought it was kind of weird, though, her going off alone. We weren't sure if it was really any of our business, but now we're kind of wondering if we shouldn't have said something earlier."

"You were right to tell me," Cole affirmed with a jerk of his chin. "When was it that you saw her leave?"

"When you guys were singing your duet,"

Whitley said. "I think it was about the time when you and Tessa—well, you know." Her face turned a bright red.

A chill ran down Cole's spine. Kaylie was in trouble. Only he and Delia knew how much, and the doctor couldn't tell anyone about it.

That was all on him.

"Here's what we're going to do," he said, quickly formulating a plan in his mind. "You tell me which way you think Kaylie went. I'll find Tessa, and we'll go after Kaylie in my truck. I want you two to find Alexis and Griff and tell them exactly what you told me. Ask them to keep their cell phones handy. I'll call them just as soon as I know anything. Oh— and bring Dr. Delia up to speed on this, too, will you?"

Whitley blanched. "You think Kaylie might be injured?"

Cole shook his head. "No. Not necessarily. But I'd just as soon cover all our bases and have the doctor available in case we need her."

Please, God, don't let Kaylie need a doctor.

Why had the girl left the barbecue? There was something very wrong with this picture. Cole could feel it in his gut.

He jogged over to his truck, which he'd parked about a block away from the community green. Soon he was headed down the dirt road in the direction he'd seen Tessa take—the one going back toward Redemption Ranch. He prayed all the way that Tessa hadn't taken any detours. She was the one person Cole completely trusted to be able to help Kaylie.

He should have told her the situation two weeks ago, when he'd first learned of Kaylie's problems. Yes, he'd made Kaylie a promise not to speak of her pregnancy to anyone, but that had been a vow he'd made in ignorance, without the full knowledge of what she was asking.

He should have gone to Tessa and Alexis immediately. He saw that now—now that it was too late.

He breathed a huge sigh of relief when he maneuvered his truck around a curve in the road and saw Tessa, still walking fast with her spine as stiff as a rod. He pulled up next to her and put his truck into Park, hopping out of the cab so he could talk to her face-to-face.

"Tessa, wait."

She didn't even bother to look back at him, much less slow her rapid pace. He quickened his step to catch up to her.

"Go away, Cole," she said raggedly. "I don't want to talk to you right now."

"This isn't about me—about us," Cole said, feeling winded not because of the pace Tessa had set for them but because his pulse was hammering double time in worry over Kaylie. "It's Kaylie Johnson."

Tessa skidded to a halt on the gravel road. Dust flew up around her feet. She swiveled to meet his gaze. "What about her?"

"She's disappeared from the barbecue. Apparently a couple of the kids saw her leave earlier, slipping out while we were singing our duet."

"And no one has seen her since?" Any personal awkwardness between them vanished as Tessa switched into full counselor mode.

"Not that I know of."

"Any guesses where she might be?"

"Not really. I'd hoped maybe I'd see her on this road, heading back to the ranch like you were."

"Maybe she is. You said she left while we were still singing. That would put her ahead of us somewhere, assuming this is the direction she took."

"My truck will be faster," Cole said gravely.

Tessa nodded and allowed him to hold the door open while she climbed in. Cole hopped into the driver's side and gripped the steering wheel with both hands as he maneuvered the truck down the road. His mind wasn't on where he was going. It was time to come clean with Tessa, and he didn't know where to begin. She was probably going to hate him after this, and he wouldn't blame her if she did.

"What's wrong?" she asked, glancing his direction. "You know something, don't you? About why Kaylie took off today?"

He nodded. "Maybe. Yes."

"Which is it? Maybe or yes?"

"Yes." There was no easy way to break this news to her, so he just clenched his jaw and forced the words from his lips. "She's pregnant."

"She's *what*?" Tessa's voice rose an octave. "How did I not know this?"

Cole was stunned. He'd just admitted to a major failure on his part and she was already blaming herself for her perceived oversight.

She turned until she was staring straight at him. "Cole—how do *you* know she is pregnant?"

There it was, then. The blame, shifting to his shoulders, as it should be.

"She—er—told me." They reached the ranch without having found Kaylie, and Cole parked the truck in front of the house. He stared at his hands still clenched on the wheel rather than meeting her gaze. "I was out riding a couple of weeks ago, and I found her in one of the pastures, sobbing her eyes out. It took a little bit of convincing on my part, but she eventually told me why she was so upset."

"And it didn't occur to you to tell me any of this?"

"Of course it occurred to me!" He removed his hat and roughly jammed his fingers through his hair. "But I couldn't."

"Why is that?" She sounded hurt more than angry. Cole cringed.

"Because she asked me not to."

"And you seriously didn't think that maybe her desire for privacy was not in her best interest?"

"She made me promise not to tell anyone and I agreed. But that was before I knew she was seven months pregnant. I thought she was going to tell me about a fight with her boyfriend or something."

"Seven months." Tessa groaned. "Oh, Cole. That poor little girl is as skinny as a rail. How could she possibly be that far along?"

"I thought the same thing," he said as they exited the truck. Even though they hadn't discussed it, they both headed straight for the girls' bunkhouse. "Dr. Delia said the baby is okay. Kaylie is underweight, but not dangerously so."

"How could I have not seen this?" The self-recrimination in her tone made Cole want to pull her into his arms and reassure her that none of this was her fault.

She had to know he was the one to blame.

"I convinced her to see Delia only because I could guarantee her doctor-patient confidentiality."

"You took her there yourself?"

Cole set his jaw. "I did. And I tried to convince her to share her burden with you and Alexis, but she didn't even want to talk about it."

"Except to you."

"And now she's taken off, so you can see all the good I did for her."

Neither one of them was thinking only of Kaylie's situation. Cole knew full well Tessa's thoughts, like his, had traveled back to the tragedy with Savannah.

He reached for her shoulders and turned her to face him. "Kaylie's not gone, Red. For all we know, she just went for a long walk to clear her head. Even if she is trying to leave town, she can't have gotten very far. We'll find her. I promise."

He allowed himself one moment just to pull her into his embrace, to let her rest her head on his shoulder. He stroked her hair, a motion as soothing to him as he hoped it was to her. She relaxed in his arms for a moment but then quickly collected herself.

"Come on," she said, reaching for his hand. "Let's check the bunkhouse."

Chapter Nine

Tessa didn't know whether to be angry or relieved when she and Cole discovered Kaylie in the bunkhouse. Tears were pouring down Kaylie's cheeks, and she appeared oblivious to them. She was packing all of her clothes into her lime-green suitcase.

"Are you planning to go somewhere?" Cole asked, leaning his shoulder against the door frame.

Kaylie jumped in surprise at the sound of his voice. "I'm leaving." She sniffled. "You can't stop me."

The expression on the teenager's face was a mixture of determination and despair. Clearly the poor child's emotions had been stretched as far as they could go.

"I wouldn't count on that," Cole countered mildly.

Tessa flashed him a desperate look. The last thing Kaylie needed right now was for someone to come down hard on her. Cole's tone had been gentle, but his words were too harsh for the situation.

Tessa knew how Cole felt. She was experiencing many of the same emotions, among them anger and fear. But now was not the time to give in to those feelings.

"You're going to be here for only one more day. Why do you think you need to leave now?" she asked.

"That's just it. My dad is going to be there to meet the van when we get back to Houston. I—" Fresh tears streamed down Kaylie's cheeks.

Tessa's immediate response was to reach out to Kaylie, but before the thought had firmly formed in her mind, Cole was already kneeling in front of the teenager, opening his arms to her and offering his strong, broad shoulder for her to cry on.

"Come here, sweetheart," he coaxed, the very picture of a father figure. A mentor. "Everything is going to be okay."

Tessa sat down on the bed beside Kaylie and put an arm around her. Cole met Tessa's gaze over the top of Kaylie's head. His eyes registered the same fear she held in her heart.

Would Kaylie be okay?

Tessa more than anyone knew there was no way of predicting what would happen, no possible way of making that kind of guarantee. Only God knew Kaylie's future—or any of their futures.

"We're not going to let you face this alone, Kaylie," Cole assured her, reaching for Tessa's hand to bring the three of them together in a circle. "You may be leaving Redemption Ranch tomorrow, but Tessa and I will stay in touch with you for as long as you need us, okay? We'll be there for you *and* your baby."

Tessa knew the words were meant to reassure Kaylie, but they worked on her heart, as well. He was supporting her as she worked through her own fear. When he squeezed her hand, she felt enveloped in his warmth and strength.

Kaylie pulled back, wiping her tears away with the sleeve of her shirt. "I'm scared," she admitted softly.

"We know you are, darlin'," Cole said. "But running away isn't going to solve your problem. It'll only give you new ones. You have to think of your sweet little baby waiting to be born."

"But my dad—what if he hates me?"

Tessa wanted with all her heart to assure Kaylie that there was no way her father could ever hate her. But how could she say those words when she didn't believe them herself?

"I know you've seen my little baby boy, Grayson," Cole said gently. "He's the light of my life, just like you are to your father. Now granted, my little tyke can't even crawl yet, but I can't imagine that there's anything he could ever do that would make me love him less than I do right now."

Tessa's heart welled so full she thought it might burst right out of her chest.

She loved this man. Really *loved* him. It was likely that she always had, but never so much as she did at this moment.

"Your father might be shocked by the news at first. Angry, even. But you are his daughter, and the child you are carrying is his grandchild. I don't know your dad, but I do know what it is to be a father."

"I never thought of that," Kaylie admitted, pressing both hands over her belly. "This is his grandchild."

Tessa could see it now, the artful way Kaylie had disguised her growing midsection with loose shirts. She couldn't imagine how she ever missed it. She'd been blind, in more ways than one.

"We're both going to support you through this," Tessa said, echoing Cole's sentiments. "I know Cole took you to see Dr. Delia. Have you thought about where you want to give birth? Do you have anyone you trust to be your birthing coach?"

Kaylie seemed to brighten when they talked about her baby.

"No. I'd like— That is, I wish I could stay here in Serendipity. At least until the baby is born. I like Dr. Delia. She delivers babies, right?"

"Yes, she does, at a hospital in San Antonio. I'm not sure how that would work out for you, since you live in Houston."

Immediately the light left Kaylie's eyes.

"You said your father is a professor, didn't you?" Cole asked, leaning back on his heels and bracing his hands on his thighs.

"Yes. He teaches philosophy at Rice."

"Does he teach summer classes?"

"No. He spends his summers reading and fishing."

"We've got quite a few good streams and lakes around here. I wonder if we could tempt your father to spend a couple of months in Serendipity. There's a nice bed-and-breakfast here in town, and I'm sure if I talked to the Howells, I could get a good deal for you and your dad."

"Tessa could be my birthing coach." Excitement filled Kaylie's voice. "I mean—Tessa, would you be my birthing coach? I trust you more than anybody. Well, except for Cole. You know what I mean."

The plan sounded perfect. Too perfect. Tessa wasn't sure Cole should be filling Kaylie's head with all of these ideas. What if her father struck them down?

Kaylie was apparently thinking the same thing. Her face fell. "I don't know…"

"I'll call and speak to your father tonight." Cole's attitude and his voice were brimming with confidence. Either he wasn't aware of Tessa's and Kaylie's reluctance or he was ignoring it. "It may be better if he hears of your pregnancy from me. I can explain the situation to him. That way he'll have a little time to digest the news and get used to the idea before you have to see him tomorrow. In fact, if he agrees to come out here, you won't even have to leave with the other kids."

"You'd do that?"

Tessa's heart acknowledged the answer to that question.

Of course he would. Because he was Cole Bishop, Righter of Wrongs, Slayer of Dragons. And Tessa didn't care one bit that she was getting all mushy and teary-eyed over it.

"I think you should hang out here with Tessa and try to relax, maybe play a game of cards or something. We don't want to upset your little baby now, do we?"

"But why are you doing this? No one has ever been this nice to me before."

"Why?" Cole grinned, setting Kaylie's world to right and Tessa's heart to fluttering. "It's simple, really. Because I'm a *mentor.*"

Kaylie stood between Cole and Tessa and waved at the other kids as the van drove away. Tessa laid a hand on the girl's shoulder.

"Alexis promised she'd feed us lunch before your dad gets here this afternoon. Why don't you go wash up and we'll meet you inside?"

Kaylie smiled and nodded, looking as happy and carefree as she had since she'd arrived at Redemption Ranch a month ago.

Things were definitely looking up for her, and Cole was glad of it.

Together, he and Tessa had made a difference in one girl's life. And that, he realized, was how a man changed the world. One life at a time.

The phone call to Kaylie's father hadn't been as difficult as he'd anticipated. After David Johnson got over the initial shock of finding out his teenage daughter was pregnant, his only concern was for Kaylie and her baby. He was understandably hurt that she hadn't come to him sooner, but he admitted that he'd probably made that difficult for her.

He was determined to change their relationship now, starting with moving to Serendipity for the summer so Kaylie could have her baby where she felt comfortable and loved.

Cole shifted his mind back to the present. Tessa was staring down the road where the van had disappeared, her expression pensive.

Cole threaded his fingers through hers. "All's well that ends well, right?"

Tessa gazed up at him, and he was surprised to discover she had tears in her eyes.

"Thank you," she murmured.

"For what?"

"You know for what."

"Kaylie? Honey, that was a tag-team effort. We did it together. And if I had had the sense of a billy goat, I would have told you about Kaylie's pregnancy long before I did. Then maybe things wouldn't have come to a head in such a dramatic way."

"Like you said—it ended well for Kaylie. But that's not what I was talking about. I meant about me."

She squeezed his hand and stared up at him with such emotion brimming in her gaze that his throat closed up. He felt like a million bucks when she looked at him that way.

As if he was a hero. Her hero. And that's all he had ever wanted to be.

"Are you and Grayson still meeting me at Cup O' Jo's for dinner tonight? We have a lot to celebrate."

They *did* have a lot to celebrate, but Cole was hoping there'd be one more very important item to add to that list of happy events.

He cleared his throat so he could speak. "Can we walk for a bit?"

Tessa glanced at her watch and smiled at him. "Sure. We have a couple of minutes before Alexis expects us for lunch."

Alexis was expecting them, all right— expecting them to be late for lunch, if they showed up at all. Cole had wanted to keep his plans a secret from everyone, but with Kaylie in the picture, he needed to make sure he'd squared things away with Alexis so she wouldn't wonder where they were.

At least if Tessa rejected him a second time, he'd have to endure the humiliation of only Alexis and Griff knowing about the proposal, rather than the whole town.

Of course, he was hoping he'd be celebrating, not slinking away in defeat. But this time he was going into it with his eyes and heart wide-open.

"When I came back to Serendipity, I never imagined the way God would work in my life. Every day I'm amazed at all the new blessings He's given me. My son. My job." He paused and reached for her other hand, pulling her close and touching his forehead to hers. "You."

"Cole," she murmured. She might have been meaning to say more, but he covered her lips with his. Then he fetched the ring box from his pocket and dropped to one knee.

She gasped and put a hand over her mouth.

He didn't know whether that was a good reaction or a bad one. But he was in too far to back out now, and he wouldn't have even if he could. His heart was pounding as he struggled to find the words to tell her what she meant to him.

"I botched this up the last time. I don't want to make that same mistake again. I love you. I've always loved you, but I didn't put your needs ahead of mine. I'm a changed man, Tessa. I hope you can see that. I want us to be together. You, me and Grayson. I want to take care of you both, and any other children we might add to our family."

"Please." Her voice was hoarse with strain. "Cole."

He jumped in before she could continue, afraid she might be turning him down before he'd even had the chance to ask the question.

"I'm getting ahead of myself again, aren't I? I want to do this right. Will you marry me, Tessa, and make me the happiest man in the world? I know that sounds cliché, but it's the truth. There is nothing in the world I want more than to be with you."

"Oh, Cole," she said, her beautiful emerald eyes brimming with tears.

This time he didn't interrupt her. It was time for him to stop talking and start listening. He just hoped she'd put him out of his misery soon, because he couldn't breathe until she answered him.

She smiled through her tears and pulled him to his feet, offering him her left hand so he could slip the glittering diamond solitaire on her finger.

"I love you, too. I want to be your wife more than anything in the world, and you know I love Grayson. I wasn't sure you would ask me again."

"I guess we have more to celebrate tonight," he said, kissing her once, and then again. He would never tire of holding her in his arms.

"Alexis!" she exclaimed, drawing in a breath. "We're late for lunch."

Cole laughed. "Don't worry about a thing, Red. I've got you covered. Every second of every day. Now and forever."

She wrapped her arms around his waist and tucked her head on his shoulder, sighing deeply. "Now and forever."

* * * * *

Dear Reader,

Welcome back to Serendipity, Texas. I'm so happy you've joined me for the third novel in my Cowboy Country series. I love my rugged cowboys and adorable babies, and hope you're enjoying the books, as well.

When I look at the world these days, it's hard not to get depressed about all the terrible evils happening around me. Sometimes I wonder how I can change the world *f*for good when there's so much bad going on. Cole Bishop feels this way at the beginning of *The Cowboy's Surprise Baby*. He's endured a rough string of events, and worse yet, his own actions have caused most of them. He doesn't believe a man like him can make a difference in the world. It takes Tessa Applewhite, a counselor at Redemption Ranch, to make him see he really can change the world one heart at a time.

Are you wondering if your life has meaning, if anything you do makes a difference? I hope *The Cowboy's Surprise Baby* will remind you that your life does have great meaning, both to God and to the world. Every kind word and action makes someone's day. I hope today my words have made yours.

I love to connect with you, my readers, in a personal way. You can look me up at www.debkastnerbooks.com. Come visit me on Facebook at www.facebook.com/debkastnerbooks, or you can catch me on Twitter, @debkastner.

Please know that you are daily in my prayers.

Love Courageously,

Deb Kastner

LARGER-PRINT BOOKS!

GET 2 FREE
LARGER-PRINT NOVELS
PLUS 2 FREE
MYSTERY GIFTS

Love Inspired®
SUSPENSE
RIVETING INSPIRATIONAL ROMANCE

Larger-print novels are now available...

YES! Please send me 2 FREE LARGER-PRINT Love Inspired® Suspense novels and my 2 FREE mystery gifts (gifts are worth about $10). After receiving them, if I don't wish to receive any more books, I can return the shipping statement marked "cancel." If I don't cancel, I will receive 4 brand-new novels every month and be billed just $5.49 per book in the U.S. or $5.99 per book in Canada. That's a savings of at least 19% off the cover price. It's quite a bargain! Shipping and handling is just 50¢ per book in the U.S. and 75¢ per book in Canada.* I understand that accepting the 2 free books and gifts places me under no obligation to buy anything. I can always return a shipment and cancel at any time. Even if I never buy another book, the two free books and gifts are mine to keep forever.

110/310 IDN GH6P

Name	(PLEASE PRINT)

Address	Apt. #

City	State/Prov.	Zip/Postal Code

Signature (if under 18, a parent or guardian must sign)

Mail to the **Reader Service:**
IN U.S.A.: P.O. Box 1867, Buffalo, NY 14240-1867
IN CANADA: P.O. Box 609, Fort Erie, Ontario L2A 5X3

**Are you a current subscriber to Love Inspired® Suspense books
and want to receive the larger-print edition?
Call 1-800-873-8635 or visit www.ReaderService.com.**

* Terms and prices subject to change without notice. Prices do not include applicable taxes. Sales tax applicable in N.Y. Canadian residents will be charged applicable taxes. Offer not valid in Quebec. This offer is limited to one order per household. Not valid for current subscribers to Love Inspired Suspense larger-print books. All orders subject to credit approval. Credit or debit balances in a customer's account(s) may be offset by any other outstanding balance owed by or to the customer. Please allow 4 to 6 weeks for delivery. Offer available while quantities last.

Your Privacy—The Reader Service is committed to protecting your privacy. Our Privacy Policy is available online at www.ReaderService.com or upon request from the Reader Service.

We make a portion of our mailing list available to reputable third parties that offer products we believe may interest you. If you prefer that we not exchange your name with third parties, or if you wish to clarify or modify your communication preferences, please visit us at www.ReaderService.com/consumerschoice or write to us at Reader Service Preference Service, P.O. Box 9062, Buffalo, NY 14240-9062. Include your complete name and address.

LISLP15

READERSERVICE.COM

Manage your account online!

- Review your order history
- Manage your payments
- Update your address

> ### We've designed the Reader Service website just for you.

Enjoy all the features!

- Discover new series available to you, and read excerpts from any series.
- Respond to mailings and special monthly offers.
- Connect with favorite authors at the blog.
- Browse the Bonus Bucks catalog and online-only exculsives.
- Share your feedback.

Visit us at:
ReaderService.com

RS15